SLOANE

Jim Brannon

VANTAGE PRESS
New York

The author of the chant on page 71 is unknown.

The chant "We All Come from the Goddess" on page 72 was written by Z. Buddapest © 1971.

FIRST EDITION

Published by Vantage Press, Inc.
419 Park Ave. South, New York, NY 10016

Manufactured in the United States of America
ISBN: 0-533-14736-0

Library of Congress Catalog Card No.: 2003096163

0 9 8 7 6 5 4 3 2 1

To my cousins, Linda and Butch Kofal, for without their love, acceptance, and support, life would have been very difficult.

Contents

Cillian's Story

Sloane's Story

One—The Beginning

The Forest stilled. Something significant was about to happen in a mean, little one-room hut, hidden but to forest creatures. One of the dark people of the forest, a female, crept to the half-open door and peeked in. Her eyes widened in the little pointy face etched with the intricate blue swirls she had received at her puberty rites. The outsider female was having a hard birth time. She remembered her first time, how difficult it had been, even with the aid of the Sisters of the Grove. The woman in her demanded she do something. *I must help.* She ran faster than a forest mouse to the Sisters of the Grove.

Only the flickering light from the smoky turf fire in the fireplace illuminated the poor room. A black pot of water was bubbling and hissing, adding to the sound of pained breathing and straining from the floor. Slyvie rested, panting not quite on the stool. Her hair was soaked with sweat and her eyes were dilated with pain. She looked at the dirt floor between her legs. "My baby can't fall in the dirt. Somebody help," she cried.

A great pain rolled through her. *This baby will be born.*

"Why am I alone?" she cried. But she knew why and that pain was as bad as the birth pain. She knew she would have a daughter, which is why she was hiding from the father. The great Mage, OD, wanted a son and had many women in this pursuit, but all brought forth girls. These he promptly killed. This would not happen to her baby.

Gr'ainne looked up from licking her puppies; she had just delivered hours ago. She needed to go to her mistress, she started to rise, a puppy whimpered, and she lay back down. Her babies needed her too.

Slyvie pulled her shift up over the bulging belly, slick and shiny with sweat. The muscles stretched to bursting and contracting like the flank muscle of a fly-bitten horse.

"Don't let me fail again," tore from her lips as another contraction rolled over her.

"Why am I always alone?" she cried again. This time the big sheep dog got up from her three nursing puppies and anxiously licked the sweat from her face. "Gr'ainne, take care of my baby."

"My baby, my baby, **MYY Baabyyy!**"

In a great scream and gush, the baby left its world and slid into this one.

She collapsed on the floor. The bleeding did not stop. She accepted her fate as women had done before and would continue to do; her first concern was for her baby.

She prayed, "Mother, I am always alone until I remember you. Take my baby for your service, and let me come home." The smoky turf fire became white healing light, filling the room. Incense masked the smell of blood and birth.

The young mother's face glowed, the pain lines gone, she felt peace and she was not alone. "Our Mother has you now, my baby." Life left her torn empty little body. As her spirit merged with the light, the intensity of the white light bloomed for an instant then faded, to hearth light the flicker fire of turf.

Gr'ainne nudged Slyvie, trying to rouse her. Gr'ainne

looked down at the bloody little form between Slyvie's legs. She tentatively licked the little head and felt something. She licked again and she heard a faint cry. Gr'ainne licked the little body clean, chewed the cord through, and carried the baby girl to her puppies' bed. There she curled up around the new life.

That is the way the Sisters of the Grove found them. The baby girl fighting for life curled up in the fur of Gr'ainne and her puppies.

"We are too late. Slyvie's spirit is in the wind. The baby?" Idun, Priestess of the Grove, cried.

"Here with the puppies. It is a female and she lives." The plump Initiate Priestess said. "Look! She is fighting for a teat. This one is a warrior."

"Then she is Sloane." Idun said, gently picking up the infant and cradling her in her arms. Thus Sloane was named and of this world.

Outside a little dark female with blue swirls on her face smiled a pointy-toothed smile and faded into the forest.

Two—The Skirniri

The Grove Sisterhood administered to the surrounding area, they midwifed every living creature. They taught the young women of the communities the mysteries of life, the secrets of nature, and the healing arts. Their shrine was an oak grove, deep in the forest, a living temple to the Goddess. The Grove was ancient; women had been coming here long before the Christian God came to these shores. Christian women still came and were welcomed and administered to. Only goodness came from the Women of the Grove.

But where there is goodness, there is always evil. And the evil in this land was the Skirniri. The Skirniri were male dominated and of a perverted social order; they believed that women were unclean and inferior; their sign was the Phallus.

This was a secret order. The people in the land never knew which men of the community might be a sympathizer of the Skirniri. The Priesthood was evident and strong. They strode through the communities, their bodies painted red and black, usually in pairs. They were pair bonded; all of the priesthood and the all the known followers were this way. They took whatever they needed, but only from females of the community, and the men of strong women.

Sloane was four when the Skirniri burst into their Grove, like screaming demons from the underworld. They killed all who stood, and all whom they caught trying to flee.

Idun and Sloane were running for their lives when Gr'ainne turned and tore the throat from a screaming, slashing, blood-lusted Skirniri.

A heart-stopping shriek stopped Sloane, and she turned to see the pair bonded red and black demon, chopping Gr'ainne down with an ax. Gr'ainne fell beside the one she had killed, her shaggy white coat red with her lifeblood. Sloane ran to her and stood over her with a small serving knife, her little face contorted with rage. She challenged the Skirniri, all of them; in the warbling tongue of the Forest Dark People, and the Skirniri shrank back, afraid of her. Idun snatched her up, and they ran through the trees blending in and becoming part of the forest, invisible to the now pursuing men.

"Why do we run? We can fight," Sloane cried. "They killed Gr'ainne."

"Gr'ainne gave her life for you, she is not sorry, she died so you might live." Idun was holding the little girl with ginger-fired hair. They were hiding in the hollow of an ancient oak. "Feel the warmth of the old spirit of the oak. It gives us shelter and comfort, that is our way, your way."

"That is not my way. I will destroy the Skirniri," Sloane said, stifling a yawn. But she was too tired from running to feel angry anymore. The last thing she remembered before she fell asleep was the feeling of Idun's warm breast against her cheek.

Three—The Island of Women

It's time you go to the Island of Women, Sloane. We need your spirit and fire and you must learn our ways. Idun cradled and rocked the little girl.

Then Idun prayed. "Goddess, we have the fiery light that will protect our Sisterhood in this Child. Permit us to wake up on the Island of Women." As they slept, the elements to time and space became one for them, and the next morning they woke up on The Island of Women.

Sloane grew in wisdom and beauty, but she never assumed the humility of the others on the island. She continually challenged and asked, "Why?"

"I get so tired of her asking why," Blayne the rail-thin Priestess of the Healing Arts said. "Sometimes I do not know why—I just accept. Why can't she?"

"See, you just asked why," Idun teased.

"You know what I mean," Blayne said.

7

"Yes, but then we are not going out in the world to find and reopen all the old shrines of the Goddess, and Sloane has been selected," Idun said.

"I think she selected herself." Blayne sniffed. "What can she do? She is but eleven. She has not even lived as an initiate yet."

"She leaves us on the full moon to go to the place of Faeries and Magic. I shall miss her, and so shall you," Idun said.

On the night of the full orange moon, Sloane accepted the embraces of the women who had come to bid her farewell. She was the only initiate. So she would live alone, learning of herself and gaining a relationship with Nature and the Goddess. In the entire history of the Island, there had never been just one initiate.

She would have only their prayers. There were specified tasks to be done, but of the most importance she must learn harmony of spirit and soul. This she could only get from the Goddess.

Idun was the last in line. She walked with Sloane down the lane silvered with moonlight. Dew on the leaves glistened like diamonds, and night creatures' eyes glowed red, green, and yellow As they walked arm in arm, the night things paused in song as they passed, so they walked in silence. "Do not fear. Your spirit is strong," Idun said, holding tightly to Sloane's arm. "I love you as if I am your Mother."

"Idun, Mother, you are my mother. You are all I know. I do not fear." Sloane stopped and wiped the tear that was running down Idun's cheek. "I will be fine."

"But your courses have yet to flow, and you will be alone. I should be there with you when you make that passage into womanhood."

"Mother, I am ready. You know how I am, let them flow and get it over with," Sloane said.

"Yes, child, but then you will be fertile—You can bear children." Idun was shaken by Sloane's irreverence for passage into womanhood.

"I want no man. I have seen no man I would take into my body. I will be inconvenienced once a month, and then I will dry up. That is all."

Idun smiled. "You have seen very few men, but one day you will see one who will quicken your blood and warm that region you say will be an inconvenience to you."

"I will be fine, Idun, do not worry. At the end of this Faerie Path is my home and I shall live there until the Goddess says I am ready to leave." Sloane turned and disappeared into the darkness, and the night creatures shattered the silence with their songs.

Four—Gwen of the Glen

Humans hadn't lived in the hut in years, but it was home to the doves that lived in holes in the thatch, with the mice and a myriad of insects. Since she was not allowed to bring anything other than the clothes she was wearing, Sloane had to fashion everything herself.

She made a tall grass broom and swept the floor clean. As she cleaned she discovered things of interest. In one corner there was a old loom, and on the mantel of the fireplace a Celtic harp.

"It must be a Faerie harp, they must know I'm here. It's a gift to me." Her little girl heart determined to return gift for gift. She removed the only thing she had of her birth mother, a throat torque. She removed the harp and set the torque in its place, it was not a good torque, it turned her neck green. But she had worn it from the time Idun, her adopted mother, gave it to her.

By nightfall she had the hut clean enough to spend the night, if it didn't rain. She had not figured out how to repair the thatch. She still had no food. But she found a fire-blackened pot and a small bowl in the ashes of the hearth.

After laboriously striking a rock against the pot to make sparks, she was finally rewarded with fire. Now she brewed a tea from some roots and thistles that she knew would rejuvenate her.

She was bending over the pot dipping out a bowl when she heard, "May I have a cup?"

Sloane did not jump, she was startled, but her body did not show it. She turned and held out her only bowl to whomever was there. "You are my guest, everything I have is yours," she said. "But where are you?"

"Right here, you are using your physical eyes, use your mind's eye. This should be easy for you, Sloane." The voice came from in front of her and was pleasing to the ear, it was female.

Sloane watched the bowl leave her hands and rise to somebody's lips, then as she heard a little throat work, a form shimmered, wavered and locked in place.

"There you are. You are beautiful, who are you?" she asked the almost transparent female figure.

"I am Gwen of this glen, this is my kingdom. My world is right beside yours. I come and go as I please." Her translucence flickered and she stood whole and radiant in front of Sloane. "You please me, Sloane. You please me with your manners, your priorities and cleanliness. And

10

you pleased me with your gift, your most precious possession, your mother's torque."

Sloane felt the warmth and light of the faerie fill the hut. "Do I bow or kneel to you, Gwen? I do not know the courtesies given a Faerie Queen."

Gwen threw back her head and laughed the laughter of wind chimes and leaves blowing in the breeze. "I like you, Sloane, Initiate of this World.—Neither. We will respect each other as friends. Soon I will show you this world of mine. You may want to live here."

"No, I have too much to learn and do here. I cannot stay long. But I do want to see your world," Sloane said.

"I give you two gifts. Here, your mother's torque. Take it back; it will not turn your neck green now. The second gift is whatever you want it to be, but remember you could jeopardize your initiate rites if you choose wrong." Gwen put the torque around Sloane's neck. She smelled of fresh rain and new flowers.

Sloane thought, then said, "I want a companion. Give me a dog with spirit and soul like Gr'ainne." *I want the thatch repaired too,* she thought.

Gwen said, "The Harp will soothe your soul when you are lonely and make peace between the Little People and the Faeries. Yours is the world between worlds, so play it often." And she was gone; the space where she had been lingering like flower scented mist in the small room.

Sloane refilled her bowl and drank deeply; she was tired after walking most of the night to get here and then working all day. She had no bed yet, so she curled up on the fireplace hearth and slept the sleep of an exhausted eleven-year-old girl.

When the light of the morning sun fell on her face through the east window, she woke. What a lovely dream. Then she felt the Torque at her throat, and smelled the

11

faint scent of new rain and fresh flowers still in the air. Perchance it was not a dream?

"Whuufff." A cool nose pushed against her face.

Sloane's laughter rang through the glen, and Gwen smiled. But Michlean, king of the little people, scowled.

"Who is living in the hut?" he demanded. But no one was listening to him.

They listened as Sloane played. She had learned at an early age to play the small Celtic Harp of the Bard. Now the magical strings of the Faerie Harp floated between the three worlds, soothing the friction sometimes created by the close proximity of each.

A smile shattered King Michlean's dour countenance. "Ah, who cares, she plays like a Angel." He leaned back in his throne, smiling.

Breasal, the Friendly, tugged on Michlean's jacket, "It is the girl child, Sloane, a Initiate of the Sisterhood of their world. Gwen visited her last night and gave her gifts."

Michlean scowled again. "Find something she wants and get it for her. We must keep her playing," he ordered.

Five—Chullain

The dog, large by wolfhound standards, was not wolfhound. He was a sheep dog. His large pink tongue lathered Sloane's face as she rolled on the ground with him. "What's your name, boy? Where did you come from? Gwen sent you? You are a faerie dog?"

When they sat up they sat across from each other, the dog's head was higher than Sloane's. "Whuufff," he said, and Sloane saw in his eyes a kindred spirit.

"Chullain, you are Chullain," she said.

"Whuufff," Chullain replied.

"You're the only male I need in my life, the only one I want," Sloane said.

"Whuufff, whuufff," was Chullain's response.

Six—The Pool and the Vision

Sloane and Chullain searched out their glen from one end to the other. Behind the hut that was becoming a home was the gorse-covered hill. Sloane, hearing water, traced the source to a hidden cul-de-sac that ran water out of the rocks and splashed into a hip-deep pool. She was delighted. A place to bathe only steps from the hut.

She stripped down and bathed, using grasses that lathered as soap. Chullain lay in the sun dozing and waking, his inquisitive brown eyes watching the antics of his new mistress with wonder. Sloane rubbed the weak lather over her body and as she scrubbed, she noticed new sensations in her breasts. She lay back in the pool as the first sensual feeling she ever experienced crept over her body.

She felt eyes watching her, and when she sat up, she saw Chullain, his head cocked to one side, watching her. "Whuufff," he said.

"Whuufff, yourself. Go watch the entrance. I don't need anyone else watching me bathe." Sloane quickly finished her bath and washed her tunic and shift. She had to lie naked in the sun while they dried on the rocks. She again felt the new feelings flood her body as the sun warmed her. She lay back, her hair spread out like a fan, arms and legs splayed like her hair, the warm sun and

13

light breeze caressed her body. She shuddered with pleasure.

In that place between sleeping and waking, she saw him. He had a high forehead, his brow shrouding his eyes, his nose almost pug, his cheeks smooth and clear, his mouth thin and straight, his chin strong. He wore his hair warrior-short. And his eyes were ice blue, cold killing eyes. He turned and looked at her. They gazed at each other, the killing eyes softened and opened wide. To her gaze.—And she woke up.

"Come, Chullain, we must go. We wasted too much time here." She pulled her clothes on. *Who was that? I did see him?*

Seven—Breasal of the Leprechauns

"What's the matter, boy?" Sloane asked Chullain. He was sitting at the entrance of the cul-de-sac, watching movement in the thatch of their home. "What is that on our roof?"

Chullain didn't seem alarmed. He jumped up and bounded toward the hut, tail wagging. He sat down at the base of the house, tongue hanging, head cocked, watching the activity.

"Don't let him get us! He is a ferocious big animal," cried Breasal, peeking out of a patch of fresh yellow thatch woven into gray weathered thatch.

"Who are you?" Sloane asked. "Chullain will not harm you."

"I am Breasal. The one who does all the work for King Michlean, Ruler of Leprechaun Hill behind your house."

14

He stood to his extreme height of thirteen inches, puffed out his chest, and tumbled off the roof.

Chullain leaned down and his big tongue lapped Breasal. "AAWWGHH, the beast is devouring me," he shouted and ran to Sloane. "Save me, mistress, save me."

The sound of Sloane's laughter brought the heads of more leprechauns out of the thatch where they were hiding. They hung over the side to see, and their little throats joined in with the laughter until the whole glen swelled with the joyous sound of childlike laughter.

Sloane picked Breasal up and set him back on the roof. "Why are you doing this?"

"King Michlean ordered me to do something for you when he heard you play the harp." Breasal said. "He also did not want to be shown up by Gwen and her gifts."

"How did you know to thatch the house?"

"I was here when Gwen asked you what you wanted. I heard your thought wish." Breasal smiled his shy little boy's smile on his old man's face.

"Thank you, Breasal." Sloane bent and kissed the little man, causing him to blush and all the others to titter and laugh.

"We wanted to put new thatch over the whole roof, but old King Mick said it cost too much," one of the other little men said. "Are you going to kiss me too?"

"No, not this time. But I will play for you, and only you, tonight," Sloane said. "Now finish the thatch and we will see what we can find to eat."

"We brought food—lots of it—it's inside," Breasal shouted.

So Sloane got a new roof, and learned of her power over men, even if they were only little men. They all ate and she played, and the three worlds of fairies, little people and humans were in harmony.

15

Eight—Sloane Becomes a Woman

The days and then weeks and months went by, and Sloane was learning about herself and all living things around her. But she felt something was missing. That something had yet to happen.

It was two full moons; two cycles and Sloane would be twelve. She laid the Harp aside, the night was magic, the moon was full and filling the glen with soft warm iridescence. Soft bannerlike clouds drifted across the sky, and every now and then, across the moon darkening the world below.

The man she had seen at the pool had visited her in dreams several times. At first she was disturbed by what she felt. But this night she decided that it was normal. She sat on a large flat rock in a copse of aspens, her knees clasped and her chin resting on them. She felt a new sensation, a slight cramping in her abdomen and between her legs. Then she felt wetness. Sloane reached down and felt the wetness, she brought her hand out to the moonlight. Two of her fingertips shone black in the moonlight.

"It is your time, Sloane. Your courses flow." A female voice. Sloane looked to the voice.

"You are the Goddess," she said. "I wondered when you would come to me. You look familiar to me, have I seen you before?"

"I am what is around you. I am all the women who love, nurse, and nurture. You have seen me in everything. I am even you." The figure moved from the shadow of the oak to the moonlight. "Come, we will remedy the flow until it stops."

The Goddess led Sloane back to the hut. There she showed Sloane what mothers have shown their daughters for ages. Sloane listened as she was administered to.

"You will find your sexuality can be powerful as a weapon or an instrument of love. Wars have been, and will be, fought over us."

Nine—Sloane, Men, and Her Powers

The Goddess finished showing Sloane what to do for the menstrual flow, and both women went back outside to bathe in the moonlight. "Men are needed in the order of things, but you must learn to tell the good ones from the bad ones. When you find one worthy of your love, love with abandon and completely."

"I have seen a man," Sloane said. "It was not a dream. We gazed at each other."

"You have a gift, Sloane, but it is not magical or su-pernatural. You can align with the elements and see and move through time and space. Once in the land that sank beneath the sea, all the priestesses of the old religion had that gift. You have made the journey of rebirth, and that is why you have been chosen to go out and take back our old shrines and teach the women the arts."

"I am just a girl," Sloane cried, "not yet with twelve years."

"You will stay on this island for a time. Learn to use the loom. Weaving cloth harmonizes you, it helps you think and will fulfill practical purposes, as you will need clothes. You must use your special talent to learn more about this man you saw. You will have to use men to ac-complish your task. He will be your tool and maybe your lover, if you wish."

"Won't he know and resist?" Sloane asked.

The Goddess smiled. "A man who really loves a

woman will do everything in his power for that woman. That is why we tolerate them. That and the pleasure they give."

"I have been feeling sensations that I have never had before," Sloane said.

"Enjoy them, Sloane. Women are really the lifelines. Men like to strut and preen when we bear a son for them. Little do they know who the father really is, but we do. We choose the line, not them. Love wisely and only those who are worthy."

Ten—The Loom

Sloane woke up sleeping under the Oak, with Chullain lying beside her. She stretched and yawned and felt the padding between her legs. "I wasn't dreaming, was I, boy?"

"Whuuffff," Chullain replied.

"Whuuffff," Sloane said. "Let's find something to eat."

After they ate they dragged the loom out, and set about figuring out how to make cloth. Chullain sat and watched as Sloane pulled on this, tugged on that, and then he galloped out the door. Sloane kept at it. She found an old ball of yarn and managed to get it on the frame. "I wonder why it is so important that I weave?" she wondered aloud.

"The sound of the shuttle and the repetitive movements will help you to think. Besides, you must have clothes when you make your journeys," a welcome voice said.

"Gwen, I need help," Sloane said.

"So Chullain tells me." Chullain pushed around Gwen and sat on the floor between them.

"Here now, take that yarn off. We will warp the loom with this." Gwen produced a yarn as green as the meadow grasses. "Aren't you going to ask me where this came from?"

"No, you are a Faerie Queen and we are friends," Sloane said.

Gwen's busy hands warped the green yarn on the loom as she spoke. "Good answer, never question friendship. True friends are rare and precious things. You will not have many, but those you do have will enrich you."

"I didn't know Faerie Queens made cloth?" Sloane was helping as fast as she learned.

"I am a woman. What matter that I am of the Faerie world? I have a family that I care for. The lives of faeries are not all about circles, dancing, and singing. There, it's done." She sat back from the loom.

"Is this cloth magic?" Sloane asked.

"Cloth made by you will warm a child. Is that magic? Magic is thought much too highly of, Sloane. Think on about what love has accomplished and what magic has done and tell me which is the more powerful?" Gwen smiled at the woman child, Sloane, as she worked the shuttle back and forth through the loom. She reached up and kissed her on the cheek, but when Sloane looked again, Gwen was gone.

Eleven—Visions in the Pool

The days, weeks, and months that followed brought changes to Sloane. She grew to her full height of five feet and two inches. She was of athletic build, with firm bosom and buttocks, and her movements were quick and

19

efficient. She had a sunny disposition that was rarely darkened with the clouds of anger. But when the storm came, it came quiet and controlled, and it was over just as swiftly.

One day as she finished bathing, she was looking at the ginger-haired girl with wide, intelligent eyes, lovely cheekbones, a sensuous mouth, and strong tapering chin. "You could be prettier," she said to her reflection and she flicked it into ripples with her fingers.

As she watched, the ripples smoothed and disappeared. At first it looked to be just a vision of stormy seas. Sloane watched fascinated. She felt something else was happening. As she watched a longboat smashed to the top of mountainous swell and caromed down the side in the angry seas. The sail was shortened, and the oars between the shields were trying to get a bite on the sea to keep the ship into the wind. The young man at the tiller was shouting and fighting the bucking helm to keep the longboat on course.

Sloane leaned over to see more clearly. "Who are you? What is your name?" she asked of the man. It was the man of her visions. She heard the sound of the canvas popping like frozen trees in winter. She heard the shriek of the wind and the bump and crash as the seas broke over the ship. The ship again broke free and rose high on the crest of the sea, then in a racing plunge disappeared down the side of another mountain of water. Suddenly she was cresting another great swell of green-gray water. All the sailors' faces seemed frozen in joy and exhilaration as they rode the storm out. The helmsman's expression changed from exhilaration to questioning, as he seemed to be looking for something. Sloane saw him look up right at her as she bent over the pool. Their gazes locked. Startled, Sloane flicked the water with her fingers again and the vision disappeared. She sat there looking at the water, wishing she could still see the Viking at the helm. But glad she couldn't at the same time.—What would he be like?

As the water smoothed over, deep in the bottom of the pool, she looked again at her reflection. She saw herself as men saw her. She saw the lust in their eyes as they looked at her, and she shivered and embarrassment colored her pink. She quickly stirred the water and stood up.

"Maybe I am pretty enough. What do you think, boy?" She asked the ever-present Chullain.

"Whuufff."

Twelve—Chullain Speaks

The little hut clacked with the sound of the shuttle being shoved through the warp of the loom. Sloane's body rocked backward and forward as she worked. Her mind was on all the shrines she had seen while pool-gazing. The Skirniri had been busy; the grove shrines had trees destroyed, altars smashed. The hillside shrines fared worse, as it was easy to push altars down the hill and burn the vegetation. Some of the ocean shrines that were in beach cliffs and caves, had not been discovered and they were still secretly used. "Where to start, and how?" she mused.

"Pick one shrine and rebuild it, then move to the next," Chullain seemed to say.

Sloane stopped throwing the shuttle. "Chullain, did you just speak to me?" She grabbed his ears and looked into his eyes.

"Not with words, but with thoughts. I don't do it often. Only when male reasoning might benefit you." Chullain's big tongue flicked up and licked her arm. "Whuufff."

"So that's all there is of it? Don't you think I would have arrived at that conclusion? Thank you, furry friend." And she hugged her companion while his tail thumped wildly on the dirt floor.

Sloane was preparing her shoulder bag, packing healing herbs and medicines. She had clothes for all the seasons now. "I think we are ready to go, Chullain, but I just don't know how we are going to make this journey, or even where for sure?" She looked at him and asked, "You got anything to say? I thought not. Where is all your wonderful male reasoning now?"

Thirteen—The Interloper

She stood in the door of the whitewashed thatched house nestled at the base of blue-and-green gorse covered hill. She stretched and marveled at the morning. "It's a Faerie morning for sure, Chullain," she said scratching the ears of a large shaggy dog that lived with her.

"And before the sun is four hours old, you will be a tangled mess." She groomed the sheep dog every day. "Come, we run, before the Faerie morning leaves us." She ran like a moor pony, her legs flashing, laughing and singing a warbling song. Chullain ran beside her, ahead of her, and circling her, his tongue flopping wet and pink.

He watched as he had been watching for days, quietly and well hidden. He should have moved on long ago. He was Merle of the Rock Isle, one-time squire of Sir

Dordar. He didn't know her name yet, but the girl held him there.

When the girl and the dog were well away, he made his way back to the top of the hill or mountain, depending how far you have journeyed and what you had seen.

This was a magical place overshadowing a magical glen. He didn't believe in the Faeries and the little people, but this place was revealing things to him that he didn't want to believe. He did believe in the goodness of God and feared the evil of the Black Arts and Sorcery. He was fleeing, hiding from Dordar, the Master Sorcerer, the ruler of the Rock Isle kingdom, which was many days of sailing from here. How he came to be fleeing for his life is unimportant as long as he makes his escape good.

Merle had to kneel and crawl beneath the jumbled stones to enter an ancient room. He stumbled on this place when he fell from the claws of the Slazoo, the feathered demon he was given to by Dordar. He was to be food for Slazoo's young, but a wind from this island blew Slazoo over this spot and the vulture lost his grip.

Merle saw the women on the island as he hung from the filthy vulture's claws, then the wind came at them and blew them to this spot. It was as if a shaft of Light and Goodness shot out of the earth there, making the Slazoo relax his grip. And he floated to the earth.

"Good morning, Mother." He addressed the stone figure of a matronly woman who if he had a living mother would have looked like her. She smiled at him; she always smiled when he addressed her.

"I watched your daughter again this morning. Sometimes I think she knows I am here." He talked to himself in this rock room, it seemed right. It was not dark but was lit with a soft warm glow. The room was alive, although nothing lived there that he knew of except himself. There

23

was a table and food; he did not question he only ate. The table was never empty, nor was it dirty or messy, and he was a very untidy young man. His sleeping pallet was always clean and made and he never did anything but sleep in it. He was never cold or hot; *this place is just like a mother who is caring for me.*

Then he heard, "She is my daughter. She is Sloane, a daughter of this Island." He heard these words in his head and was terrified, all the weeks he had been here and he had heard nothing. Merle put his fingers in his ears, but the words still resonated in his senses.

"Do not be frightened. We have watched you and know your heart. Sloane must journey and you must accompany her."

"But I am hunted by Dordar of the Rock Isle." he said.

"You will resolve that along the way. Now you must find a way off this Island for you and Sloane." These words were of no comfort to Merle.

"Where will I find a ship? Am I to remain in this cave? Why must I do this? Use your magic." He was directly in front of the stone woman who did not look as kind and motherly as he had thought and the smile was not quite as large.

"Magic occurs in the hearts of people. When you find the ship, you will have done part of the magic. You may continue living in this cave.—It does not become you to whine." Again the words in his head brought no comfort, as that figure was definitely no longer motherly and not smiling.

That evening just before the light of the day ran out, he heard the shuttle on the loom cease clacking. Then the plaintive sounds of the Celtic Harp sent a shiver up his spine. As he watched, Faeries materialized on the hill. They were nebulous at first, and then they appeared, as real as the leprechauns standing around him. *Leprechauns, Faeries. Merle, you're dreaming.*

"Lad, if you're dreaming, so am I, but isn't it the most lovely thing you ever heard?"

The speaker was knee high, and he had a crown of shiniest gold. His eyes snapped fire, and he waved his cudgel. "Gold, is it? Is that is all you can think of, when beauty of the harp is caressing your tone-deaf mortal ear?"

"Ssshhhhh," came from a dozen little lips, shushing them up.

"Look at the faeries dancing in their circles, silly things. Normally we don't have any dealings with faeries. Still don't, but we do come out together when Sloane plays.—Come over here with me." The little man whispered loud enough for a little shout. He reached up, got hold of Merle's finger, and led him away.

"Sit here. Introductions first. I am, if you don't already know, King Michlean of the Glen Leprechauns. And you are Merle last of the Rock Isle. I am right about you. Aren't I, boy?" They sat in the moonlight on the start of a low stone fence. The faeries were floating and gliding in their Faerie Ring. The leprechauns, obeying the call of the harp, were swaying slowly with a reel or breaking into a wild foot-flying jig.

"Why are you showing yourselves to me now when you know I don't believe in faeries or leprechauns?" Merle asked.

"Ow! Why did you do that?" He rubbed his leg where Michlean had struck him with his walking stick.

"Did that **really** hurt? We are **real**, and you are going to need us to help Sloane." King Michlean said, smacking his shillelagh in the palm of his hand. "Do you want to **really** listen now?"

"Yes, I'll listen, but I don't see what you leprechauns can do to help." Merle continued rubbing his leg and eyeing the cudgel in King Michlean's hand.

"No wonder Dordar wants to kill you. You are stupid even for a mortal." King Michlean walked away in disgust. "I don't suppose a ship would help anybody get off an island?"

"A ship? You say a ship?" Merle ran after the little king and fell on his knees both hands clasped in subservient supplication.

The harp died out, the last chord stuck, and the Faeries whisked away. The leprechauns trudged down a path that Merle had not noticed before. "Please, King Michlean, tell me of the ship," Merle pleaded.

"Not tonight. The magic is over. You mortals make my belly hurt. Go away." Michlean, the leprechaun king, moved imperiously past Merle, but another leprechaun stopped him and whispered in his ear, all the while looking back at Merle who was still on his knees. King Michlean threw up his hands and Merle heard a string of profanity that made the other leprechaun with him cover his ears. Then King Michlean continued on down the leprechaun trail.

"I am Breasal. I am the Doer Leprechaun, and I get things done." Breasal assumed his puffed-out chest pose.

Merle got up, brushed off his knees and while bent down reached out to shake the leprechaun's hand. "Glad to meet you, Breasal. What's this about a ship?"

"There is one beached and battered. It washed ashore months ago," Breasal said. "I can show you tomorrow."

"Show me tonight."

"No, mortal. You are in our land now. Go back to your hole in Faerie Mountain."

Merle saw only a flash as Breasal fled down the trail.

Fourteen—Sloane Meets Merle

"Now, by all that is good here, what do I do?" Merle asked the moon, which was smaller and less luminous, but seemed the only friend he had at the moment.

"You may sleep on the floor in my house." A voice turned him around, his breathing stopped on the intake, and his face started to glow from the strain.

"You better breathe, Merle. It is required to live." Sloane stood behind him, her ginger-red hair black in the dim light, but flowing around her face, framing it and sealing the vision in Merle's heart forever.

Whhooossh and uunngh, the breath left and reentered his chest loudly and noticeably. "You startled me," he said. "How do you know me?"

"We've known about you since we caused Slazoo to drop you." Sloane smiled and reached for his hand. " Now you won't have to hide and spy on me. Come I have some tea. It will not be as good as you have been drinking, but it is good."

Her hand felt strong and warm. Merle immediately thought the thoughts of a fourteen-year-old male, and his palm began to sweat.

"That is not going to happen, Merle," Sloane said, without removing her hand.

"Oh, I didn't say anything." Merle was glad it was dark, so Sloane couldn't see his red face and especially the front of his trews.

The little hut had a cheery peat fire going in the hearth with a pot gently steaming a spicy aroma. Merle looked at Sloane's neat bed in the corner and quickly looked away.

"Here, Merle. Drink." Sloane handed him her drinking bowl; he drank and handed it back. She smiled and drank from the same spot on the bowl. Merle shivered visibly and shook his head no, when she handed the bowl back.

"I'll sleep outside," he stammered.

"No. You take Chullain's bed and he will sleep outside."

Merle lay down in the cloth scraps while Chullain watched, his eyes more soulful than ever.

Sloane chuckled her low, and to Merle's ear, unbearably titillating laugh. "So sad you are, Chullain. You can sleep with me tonight."

Chullain's soulful look turned triumphant. He stepped through his rag bed, brushing Merle and switching his tail across his face, he leaped into Sloane's small bed.

In one quick fluid motion, Sloane pinched out the small oil lamp, slipped her tunic over her head, hung it on a peg on the wall, and slipped into her bed.

Merle glimpsed in that flash in the dim light of the peat fire, the only woman he would ever really love. All women would now be held to her standard and found lacking.

Sloane heard a small groan from the boy in the dog's bed and wondered, but said nothing.

Morning came too soon for Merle. "Come. Eat," Sloane said. She had laid out a bowl of thin watery cheese and a chunk of bread.

"What do I wash this down with?" Merle asked. His hair was in his eyes, and sleep was still visible in them. His cheek still bore the creases from the rag bed.

"Water," was her answer. "Why don't you use some on yourself before you come to the table?"

Merle picked at the fare, his stomach growling. "I ate

better that this in Dodar's dungeon," he muttered. "Didn't have someone nagging either."

"So our mortal friend's stupidity of last night is magnified by his lack of graciousness this morning." There in the doorway stood King Michlean and the Doer Leprechaun Breasal. "Sloane, are you sure you need this dunce?"

"Yes. He has knowledge of ships and sailing."

"How do you know this? Even Slazoo did not want him."

"Where is this ship? I am smart enough; you do not need to talk around me. That is not polite either," Merle said. "I've had quite enough of being found lacking."

"He's right. We are not being polite," Breasal said.

"I am King Michlean. I do not have to be polite, especially to mortals," Michlean said.

Fifteen—The Ship

Breasal led Sloane and Merle across the heather moor, and through the peat bog. Each step brought the sound of the sea, the clarion call of a sailor or traveler. They came to a jumble of wind and water-battered rocks. The salt and seaweed smell was compelling them to take the other step.

Then, through a break in the rocks, the frothy gray-green sea at low tide was visible. Gulls screeched their welcome as they flew overhead. Diving birds plummeted into the sea rising on wet struggling wings, then back into the air with a shiny fish in their beaks. From the rocks the seals barked their welcome.

Sloane ran ahead turning in little circles with arms

outstretched in joy. "Good morning, Silkies! Good morning, Birds! Thank you, Goddess, this is wonderful."

Merle looked at the leprechaun. Breasal looked back and shrugged. It was a nice morning, but he didn't feel like running and skipping after walking all this way.

"There it is," Breasal said, pointing at the bow of a small knarr, partially buried, with the hull holed just at the water line. Some of the planking was sprung, and the mast had slipped from its step, leaning precariously.

They walked to the ship. Merle walked around it, examining it with the eye of a sailor. For even with only fourteen years of age, before he went to Sir Dordar as squire in training, he lived and sailed with his father, a renowned sailor of the northern seas.

"This is no ship; this is a wreck," he announced.

Sloane went to him; she faced him squarely, putting both hands on his shoulders. "Can you repair and sail this ship?"

"I know how to repair her, and I can sail any ship, but this is beyond one man, a woman and a leprechaun," Merle said.

"What do you need?" Sloane asked. "Breasal, listen to what Merle says and supply everything needed. I will pay."

"How will you pay? Old King Mick does not like this mortal much and he will ask a high price."

"I can pay in cloth and music, and most of all with gratitude," Sloane said.

King Michlean bargained long and hard, but he knew he was going to give Sloane what she requested when he started the haggling. The leprechauns supplied the list of oak planking, ropes, and tar, and Merle started the daunting task of repairing the ship.

Sixteen—Repairing the Ship

Sloane had the task of weaving a new wardrobe for King Michlean, part of the payment. When this was finished, she also had to make a sail. Then, whenever Merle needed extra hands, she had to drop what she was doing and be those hands. And since she was the woman, she saw to it that they ate. Merle was of the impression he was doing all the work. Sloane let him believe that; it seemed to make him happy and kept him working and tired at night.

"Merle, come on down. I have cheese and bread," Sloane shouted from the beach.

From inside the hull, Merle answered, "Did you bring any wine, or is it water again?" His scowl disappeared when he looked down and saw Sloane. She stood in small tidewater pool, her legs apart. Her tunic came to mid-thigh, showing the sun-browned thighs that caused Merle to stammer.

"No, it's still water, good clear faerie spring water. Come on down and we will eat together." Her grin as she turned and stepped away shot pleasure pains through Merle and he leaped over the side, falling rather clumsily to hands and knees. *I'm glad she didn't see that.*

"Get up, Merle. We'll sit over here on that big flat rock." Sloane did not turn around, just set the food out for them.

Merle stood up and brushed the sand and pieces of seaweed from his hands and knees. He even pushed his hair out of his eyes; he knew that Sloane put great stock in cleanliness. They sat together in the warm sun, the salt breeze riffling the water pools where the wading birds were also feasting. The silkies were silently soaking up the sun. Every now and then, one slid off the rocks with a splash. It was a sensual time, and Merle enjoyed it. Sloane felt it too; deep inside it was warm and comforting.

"Why don't you and the sisterhood use your magic to get a good ship?" Merle asked, through a big mouthful of bread and cheese, interrupting the moment.

"I could understand you better if your mouth was not full," she scolded. "Magic cannot create; it takes a conscious effort on someone's part to put into motion anything that can be called magic." Sloane watched the boy gobble the food with affection. She felt older and sisterly toward him, for he was the first human male in her life.

Merle looked up with cheese and bread crumbs all over his face and he took a large swallow of water. The rise and fall of his Adam's apple caused Sloane to giggle. Merle didn't know what she was laughing at, but it was contagious. Soon they were both laughing uncontrollably.

The laughter subsided and Merle self-consciously slid down off the rock. "Better get back to work," he mumbled. "The hull should be finished tonight. I'm going to sleep on the ship tonight."

Sloane slid down beside him, brushed some bread crumbs off his cheek, and kissed him there. "Thank you, Merle." And she ran up the beach back to her loom.

Merle stood, his fingers touching the spot her lips had just left, he watched her young body as it flew over the jumbled rocks—one slip and she could fall, possibly to her death. "I love you, Sloane," he said as she flew off the last rock and out of view.

Merle climbed back aboard the knarr. He was starting to fall in love with the little ship, too. "You came from the frozen sea, didn't you, girl? We got the hole in your belly closed up, and after the caulking, you will look feisty again." The smaller than average ship called a knarr by the Norse, was a miniature of the fearsome Long Boats.

Long after the sun had set, Merle curled up in his new love, one that would return his love, and fell asleep. He was tired and dirty but promised himself he would bathe in the morning, before Sloane arrived.

Seventeen—The Moor Pony

Merle dreamed of Sloane, the time when he watched her dig the peat she used for heat and cooking. She and Chullain trekked to the bog; she had a peat spade over her shoulder, and she talked and sang to Chullain as he pulled a two-wheeled cart. At the bog she hitched up her skirts and her strong sun-browned legs and arms worked the spade like a man.

She cut out the spongy turf, stacking it in oblong shapes in the cart. This was an all-day and dirty affair, and after a long bath at the pool, she went to bed early. But this night the Moor Pony woke her for a night ride.

Of all her animals, and she had many, the largest was the Moor Pony. The pony came and went as he pleased. He showed up at the times when it was right for moonlight rides across through the bog and moors to the sea coast. And tonight was such a night. There they galloped across the small moon-magicked beach. Sloane sat on the pony bareback, her bare legs gripping the barrel sides of the little horse, her shift pushed up over the top of her thighs. The wind had her hair flying and her bodice pushed tight against her breasts. She felt as if she was flying.

Merle heard the whinny and the joyous laughter. He looked over the gunnels and saw Sloane head back, arms spread wide, hair billowing behind, her eyes blind to all except the joy of the moment. They galloped past and then soared into the night sky, a shower of fiery particles raining to the ground after them. Merle watched the fiery trail for as long as he could see it then sat down again.

"I love a Goddess," he said. "Where is it a dream and where is it not?"

Merle worked the rest of the night. He finished the hull and readied the mast to be stepped in place. A regular knarr required forty oarsmen; this ship was smaller and looked to seat eighteen to twenty. "But we will use sail, and if there is no wind, we wait for it." Merle talked to himself as he did when he was living in the cave.

Merle was asleep and filthy when Sloane found him at midday. She let him sleep; she didn't know for sure what she felt for him. She was grateful, but it went beyond that. She was not used to feelings and emotions concerning the male gender.

She sat for a while and watched him sleep, her thoughts drifted to the short-haired warrior who haunted her. Merle was nothing like him, but she could love Merle, and she did. But she wanted the ice-eyed one. She nodded off and they both slept.

Eighteen—Shellfish on the Beach

The next morning Merle prepared to set the mast, a tricky job. He rigged a line to the masthead and ran it to the top of the cliff, there he and Sloane pulled. The mast came up inches off the deck; they secured the haul line and rested. "We need a little more help," he said.

Chullain volunteered, "Whuufff."

And Sloane shouted, "Yes. Merle, Chullain will help."

The next time they heaved together and the mast came up slow, slow then with a jump and a bump swaying violently and rocking the ship, it fell in the mast step.

They were too winded to cheer but they hugged, grinned, and panted, lying across each other on the cliff top.

Merle built a small fire on the beach; he was roasting shellfish. Sloane sat and watched. "Tonight I cook and you eat," he said.

Merle brought a half a dozen shellfish on an old plank from the knarr and set them opened and steaming in front of Sloane. "Eat, and drink, this is not water. This is some wine I got from Breasal."

Sloane was enjoying the attention, and she smiled often at Merle as she ate. The wine heightened her senses and the color of her cheeks. She was radiantly beautiful. The little driftwood fire snapped and popped, sending green-and-blue sparks high in the air. Matching the sparks starting in the bellies of the young Merle and Sloane, as they exchanged looks across the fire.

Chullain, sensing something, left the fire and walked into the dark.

Sloane watched as Merle walked from his side of the fire to hers. She could see he was visibly aroused. *Do I want this?*

Merle sat beside her and took one of her hands in his. Sloan saw the shine of shellfish still on her fingers, "No, let me wash first," she said, jumping to her feet and running to a tidewater pool.

"Always washing, always washing," Merle muttered.

Nineteen—Dordar of Merle's Past

Behind her the moon shone down on the pool, she saw her face in the pool shatter as she splashed her hands in the water. She rocked back and dried her hands in the air and on her tunic. *I am not ready for this; I do not want this with Merle.* Sloane looked back in the moonlit pool; maybe she would be able to see what this night's outcome would be.

Merle came over to the pool after looking at his hands and seeing more than shellfish on them that needed washing off.

"Merle, is that Dordar?" Sloane asked.

"Where is Dordar?"

"Look in the pool," Sloane said.

In the black water of the tidewater pool Merle saw, he blanched, and fell to one knee. The pool vision showed a waterfront full of warships of the dromon style. Troops and horses were being loaded on to them with one man directing the operation.

Dordar strode the dockside, shouting orders; he had a command of men that seemed easy, his leering smile and wicked laughter quick and ready. "Wine!" he shouted.

A serving slave rushed forward with a tankard, and in his haste, wine sloshed out and a few drops sprinkled Dordar's boot. Dordar looked at the wet spots on the boot. The slave, stricken, fell to his knees and began wiping the boot.

Dordar drained the tankard, he threw it in the water and bent down helping the terrified slave stand up. He smiled that slow easy smile of his. The serving slave knowing what was coming next, collapsed again. But Dordar caught him, and when he turned the slave

36

around, his entrails fell to the dock. The slave took one step, tangled his feet in his own guts, fell to the dock, and twitched his life away.

"Clean this quickly and return it," Dordar ordered, handing his disemboweling knife to another slave.

"That's Dordar," Merle said.

"This will be an easy conquest, nothing but women on this island. Sport for the men, but my old squire Merle is my entertainment.—Get this refuse off my dock," Dordar ordered one his lieutenants.

"Yes sir, feed the Slazoo, sir?" the officer asked.

"Aye, feed Slazoo," Dordar said, put two fingers to his lips, and blew a shrill whistle. Out of the sky, the Slazoo swooped. Never landing, he beaked the body and rose back in the air, entrails dangling and spraying those beneath.

"That's Dordar, and he is coming here," Merle said, all thoughts of Sloane wiped from his mind.

Twenty—Merle Remembers

"We must get the sail on and the ship floated. How will you get the ship in the sound?" Sloane asked. "If we can leave, the island will move and he will not find it.—I'm going to finish the sail, you get the ship floated." She gave him a quick peck on the cheek. "Thanks for the supper. Now get the ship floating. Come, Chullain." She and the dog ran out of the moonlight and into the darkness.

Merle sat by the pool, feeling frightened and alone. He felt the evil of Dordar again, something he had almost forgot. He had been the knight's squire for two years, caring for his arms and training for his own spurs. If he hadn't opened that forbidden door that night, he might possibly still be his squire. He had never seen such a spectacle or smelled the odor of so much evil.

"I don't even want to remember that night," he said to the dying fire. But the memories, the terrifying memories, came back in waves, smashing through his mind. He saw again the banquet table. A luxurious table with gilded plates and goblets, he saw the main course. The little bodies roasted whole and slow so the eyes remained open and undamaged. The remembrance brought up the shellfish, and his body racked heaving until nothing came.

Merle lay on his back, looking to the stars. The evil that Dordar worshiped and represented had to be stopped. He had remained hidden during that vile feast. When all had left and he was trying to slip back to his room, he opened the wrong door. He stepped into a yellowish-green, sulfurous cloud, and in the center of this evil, amid terrible inhuman groaning and gasping he saw Dordar appeasing the Dark Devil Skirnir, whom he served.

Merle still trembled, remembering the look. The look that Dordar, naked, under that writhing evil entity, gave him; when he realized they were being watched. How his face changed, the slow knowing smile and the way his body matched the movements of the thing on him. Merle broke and ran from the room, he fled into the waiting arms of Dordar's disciples. His body and mind underwent horrors and torment his mind would not let him remember. But he did this night, until, trembling with fear and exhaustion, he passed out.

Twenty-one—Leprechaun Help

As the sun warmed him, it seemed the light washed the horror away and he stood to the morning sun resolute. Dordar and his disciples would not get him again.

"All I have to do is get the ship to the water, or the water to the ship," he said aloud. It seemed a daunting task, but Merle started digging a trench from the knarr to the sea. The closer to the sea, the wetter the sand was. Every scoop out caused the sides to slide back in. Merle was about to give up when he heard them.

"Well, stupid mortal, do you think a leprechaun, or three hundred leprechauns, can help?" King Michlean stood hands on his hips, his shillelagh leaning against his right leg.

"King Michlean, probably only leprechauns can save this day and get our ship floated." Merle said not feeling so alone anymore. "We can't use magic, though."

"Stupid mortal, that is why there are three hundred of us. Breasal, get them digging." And the King of the Glen leprechauns strode over to a large rock and sat imperiously.

Twenty-two—Gwen's Assistance

Sloane had finished weaving the cloth and now she was stitching the panels together to form the large square sail. She sang as she worked; her voice was pleasant and soothing.

"You have a mother's voice. You will be a wonderful mother."

Sloane knew the voice, and she smiled her gladness

at it. "Gwen, you have been gone too long. I have missed you. And I will never be a mother."

"You will be a mother, Sloane. And it won't be in your timing." The Faerie Queen knelt and put her arms around the young Sloane. "You would have made a wonderful Faerie Queen after me, but you have many adventures ahead."

Their hands flew and the sail took shape. Gwen talked of many things that Sloane needed to know, about magic, about womanhood, and about men. Sloane listened and marveled at life and what was expected of her and all women.

"Done," Gwen said. "Get this down to the ship. You will sail tonight."

"Tonight?"

"Yes, the moon is right. There will be the highest tide yet and your ship will float," Gwen said.

"Then this is the last time I will see you?" Sloane asked.

"No, dear, didn't you listen? My world is next to yours, and soon you will cross over and back like I do. You should have been the next Faerie Queen, but for the task the Goddess has set before you. Now go, put the sail on the cart for Chullain." Gwen hugged Sloane and pushed her out the door.

Twenty-three—The *Caoimhe*

King Michlean and the leprechauns had all returned to their world, the faeries were tight in theirs; they knew that the harp would not sing this night or any night soon.

Merle was making last-minute checks of rigging,

40

sail, and helm. Sloane was stowing provisions. Chullain was sitting at the mast, his head cocked, and watching everything.

"Sloane, daughter, over here." Sloane looked over the side. Idun stood there.

"Idun, Mother, we are leaving soon."

"Sloane, I have a gift, The Huntress's Bow. Here catch it." Idun threw the package over the side, and it fell with a clatter.

Sloane leapt over the side and rushed to the woman who raised her; she threw her arms around her, and they hugged as should mother and daughter, saying good-bye.

Idun pulled away. "Go, Daughter. It is your destiny. Go." She disappeared into the darkness. "We will be together again." The words floated out of the night blackness of the rocks.

Sloane, sobbing softly, took Merle's hand and climbed back into the ship.

The night became as daylight, the moon set right over the cliff. It hung larger than the cliff itself, and the wind was a steady pressure coming in off the sea. It was quiet. The slap of the halyards, and snap of the furled canvas, was hardly heard as the wind carried it inland.

Then they heard it, and felt it. The slap of water against the hull and a gentle tilting of the deck. Merle put a long push pole over and pushed. The deck righted and the ship floated, Merle pushed them through the rocks and to deeper water.

"Sloane, we row now."

There were seats for eighteen oarsmen, but Sloane and Merle, sitting side by side, put the little knarr in the sound. There they hoisted sail and tacked out of the island's cove.

"She is gentle, she has beauty and grace. This ship is the *Caoimhe*," Merle said.

"Yes, she is all that," Sloane said, tears running down her face as her island faded into the mists of the night and time.

Sloane and Chullain lay together and slept, Merle pointed the *Caoimhe* at the North Star and dozed at the helm.

* * *

Dordar, Sorcerer of the Rock Isle's Fleet, was also sailing north. They were weeks, maybe days depending on the wind, from the *Caoimhe*. The closer they would sail to the Island of Women, the farther they would be from it, since Merle was no longer there. Dordar spread havoc and destruction on every ship and island they came across. Burning ships and bodies feeding the beasts of the sea marked their course.

* * *

There was another fleet, sailing from the frozen fjords of Chieftain Ivar, the Ice Heart and Gunnarr, the Cruel. These Norsemen were on a Viking, raiding to the south, their long boats with as many as eighty fighting oarsman. These were the fiercest warriors in the world, Christian or Pagan. And in between these two fleets sailed the *Caoimhe*.

Twenty-four—The Fog Vision

A great cold, clinging, cloying oppressive fog enveloped the *Caoimhe*. Merle was visibly down. Sloane felt the danger in the wet mists; she sat, her arms around Chullain.

"Sloane, we have to find out where we are. I feel the danger and it is close," Merle said.

Sloane said nothing, she was gazing into the faint orb of the sun whose outline was barely seen through the fog. Chullain's ears twitched up, and Merle looked and saw the panorama of the sea unfolding against the backdrop of the fog and burnt-out sun. The fleets wavered and flickered, then steadied out and they were looking in a window of time and space.

"Dormons of Dordar and the others are the long boats of the Norsemen," Merle said.

But Sloane was gazing at one long boat; the picture narrowed, then widened out on a young Norseman. "It's him." She gasped.

"Who is that?" Merle asked.

Sloane did not answer. She just looked, trying to see everything she could about him.

*   *   *

"Cillian, what do you see? What are you looking for?" Ogurr, second in command and son of Gunnarr, shouted.

The Norseman turned and shouted, "I feel something out there."

"Get to the mast head then and look. Tell me what you see," Ogurr ordered. "I'm going to have to kill that boy yet," he muttered.

Perched on the masthead, Cillian looked at all points, then he looked up, and froze. His mouth opened to shout, but he closed it and gazed intently at Sloane of the ginger-fired hair. Then he shouted, "Deck," and Ogurr looked up. Cillian pointed due south.

All the long boats steered on Cillian's directions. The

Caoimhe was still between the Dormons of Dordar and the long boats of Ivar and Gunnarr.

*   *   *

On the lead ship, Dordar also sensed something, "He is not on the island, he is on a ship. Close!—**You! Come here!**"

A resting oarsman stood and tentatively approached; to be noticed was not good. He stood in front of Sir Dordar, afraid and trembling.

"There, do not be frightened. You will not be harmed." Dordar looked him over feeling his shoulders, "You are strong, good." He walked behind him, prodding his back muscles. When he came full circle and stood in front again, the oarsman had relaxed and was smiling. This might be good; he might get a reprieve from the oar.

Dordar smiled his slow engaging smile, his right hand on the man's shoulder. With his left, he brought the disemboweling knife up, and the oarsman's smile faded as he felt his intestines fall around his ankles.

Dordar quickly squatted and sifted through the entrails of the living man to foresee the future. "Pah! I see nothing. Keep the course north." He put two fingers to his lips, and his shrill whistle brought the heavy feather sound of Slazoo.

Those on deck scattered to make room, and the ship slowed with the weight of the bird, as it squatted, tearing the oarsman's head off in the first bite. Three wet tearing gulps and the man was gone. Heavy wings beat, striving for lift, and Slazoo lumbered back into the air.

Back on the *Caoimhe,* Sloane said, "Enough." The fog closed over the vision and they were again encased.

Twenty-five—*Caoimhe* in the Norse Fleet

Chullain nosed Sloane for attention, as Merle asked, "What are we to do?"

Sloane, the young woman of the Order of the Island, looked at her dog, then at Merle, who was to help her. She did not feel the fear they felt. She felt the power of never knowing defeat. She felt the power of good, and the power of the women on the island. "There is nothing to fear. The Norse are to the north. Dordar is to the south. We get out of the way and evil destroys evil." *Not Cillian please, not him. Please, Goddess.*

Merle shortened sail so they would not blunder into the force from the north or the force from the south. They watched from bow and stern, alert and listening.

"We will hear them before we see them, keep all your senses sharp," Merle said.

Sloane grinned at him. "Yes Captain."

Merle grinned back. "You know what I mean."

Sloane stood on her toes and brushed her lips across his cheek. "Yes, I know what you mean, Merle. You will get us out of this."

The *Caoimhe* luffed along for two nights and one full day. Then on the second day they heard oars in their locks and muffled voices. Before they could tack, they were sailing through the Norse fleet.

The fierce serpents' heads loomed over their small craft like mythical dragons. The oars between the shields, digging the water on either side, rocked them like a leaf in a rainstorm. The sound of the threshing oars was deafening after the muffled silence of the fog. Water splashed over the low gunnels of the *Caoimhe* and was soon ankle deep.

"Bail, Sloane, bail," Merle shouted, as he frantically threw water over the side.

The fleet passed almost as rapidly as it had appeared. "Come about, Merle. Stay with them," Sloane yelled, already tacking the sail.

Twenty-six—Sea Battle

The *Caoimhe* fell in astern of the last long boat. Sloane and Merle sat on the bench at the tiller drinking a warm tea that Sloane had brewed. It was night, the air was chill, so Merle put his arm around her.

Sloane snuggled closer to him and gave him the little smile that Merle had learned meant a thank-you and nothing more.

"When will the Dormans and the long boats sight each other?" Merle asked.

"By daybreak, we will be in a great battle. This is a certainty. I have seen it," she said.

"Battle. They will not pass each other?" Merle asked.

"Battle. When they see each other. That is their nature." Sloane pulled away and stood. "The fog is lifting. See, to the left, the sun."

Then they both heard it. The muttered cries in two languages wafted back to them. The fierce shouting rose to a crescendo, and then rolled into the sound of a large crowd on a festival day.

"Whuufff." Chullain called their attention to the sea and objects in it. A darker-skinned corpse of Dordar's fleet drifted by. Now they were passing them in twos and threes, men and horses. The teethed fish of the sea were feasting on them as they were threshing the water, leaving great cloudy red spots and gouts of flesh in the sea.

"Look," Merle shouted. A Dormon and a long boat were in an embrace of death as the Dorman went down by the bow taking the grappled long boat with her. The Norsemen were frantically trying to cut the grappling ropes, but to no avail. The sea swallowed the two angry ships, leaving a large silent bubble ring, and bobbing up in it flotsam and bodies.

"Steer to the shouting," Sloane ordered, and Merle put the helm over to the east a couple of points.

They passed crippled and sinking ships as they threaded their way through the charnel sea. "There, Sloane, there," Merle shouted.

Sloane was already looking. She had been searching each Norse face in the water for the face of her visions. Two Norse ships were secured to Dordar's dorman; but the only battle was between two warriors amidships. The rigging was filled and the decks crowded with Norse spectators. The warriors of Dordar, except for the one in red circling the young Viking, were all dead.

"That's Dordar," Merle said. "And there is Slazoo."

Circling, big wings, riding the thermals, was the hated Death Bird of Dordar. He flew above the fighting, awaiting the shrill whistle of his master.

Sloane said nothing. She was riveted to the fight; the one fighting Dordar was her Norseman. His helm was gone, and the left side of his face ran red. Dordar seemed fresh; he was light on his feet, skipping in short sword range and the short sword flicking red every time it struck.

Cillian circled warily. He wore no armour, and he bore red leaking wounds from his shoulder, side and both legs. He had called for this combat, and the Norse would honor the rules of single combat and not interfere. Cillian held an Irish fighting ax lightly in his right hand; his left held the small target. He felt no real fear. This man was a worthy opponent. He felt his strength flagging as Dordar's evil flicked at his mind. Cillian wiped at his left eye to clear the blood.

Seeing this opening, Dordar sluiced forward with fluid serpentine grace, and his short sword struck, flashing towards Cillian's throat. His stroke rang on the target as Cillian blocked the blow. Dordar reversed and spun around. The Scythian dagger in his other hand sliced a long red streak across Cillian's ribs.

Sloane cried out from the *Caoimhe,* and not only Merle and Chullain heard. Cillian heard, and the goodness and purity sealed his mind to the evil that was sapping his strength and will.

Cillian's Irish ax flashed once and cut Dardor across the back of the knee as he had reversed. Dardor's triumphant look turned to horror as he took a step and the leg crumpled under him.

"Are you ready?" Cillian asked, as he stepped forward, both hands on the ax helve.

Dardor put two fingers to his lips; the shrill whistle hailed his feathered death. Slazoo folded his wings and dove to the deck of the conquered Dormon. The shriek of the giant bird and the whistle of his plummeting flight caused Cillian to step back. The Norse archers loosed their shafts at the gigantic bird that stopped his dive at mast height and, cupping his wings, settled on deck. Slazoo's body was studded with arrows. He took a lurching step to Dordar intent on picking him up and carrying him away.

Sloane, in the *Caoimhe,* took the only weapon they

possessed, the small bow of the Huntress and knocked their only arrow.

"It's too far, it won't kill at this distance," Merle said.

Slazoo focused in on Cillian as the only threat he saw. One big talon encircled Dordar in preparation to lifting off, and his massive head started its downward killing arc to behead Cillian.

Sloane loosed her tiny shaft; it arced up with a flash like a meteor and lanced into the cold yellow eye of Slazoo.

"**AAARRRAAAWWW!**" he screamed.

Dordar felt the big talons convulse and rip through his body.

Cillian, seeing his opportunity, stepped forward and brought his ax down on the snakelike neck where it protruded from the feathered shoulders of the flying death. Three times the ax fell each time the head drooped lower. On the third cut, the gruesome head fell free at its own feet. Dordar, dying, saw his beloved pet with one eye pierced by an arrow of Athena, a woman's arrow. Even now he gloated, "Raider, you would not have this victory but for a woman. Look you the arrow in Slazoo's eye."

Cillian's mouth tightened, and his shoulders flexed, and with a little grunt, the loosed ax flashed one more time. Dordar's head, in great gout of blood, rolled beside Slazoo's. They seemed to admire each other, Dordar still wearing his smile. Cillian side-kicked Dordar's head and it rolled the length of the ship, then he pulled the arrow from the yellow eye that no longer glowed with evil life.

While the Norse finished their looting, and cheering their victory, Cillian quickly scaled the mast, and just before they slipped back into the fog bank, he saw the ginger-haired girl who had been haunting his dreams. She stood in a small knarr, with a great shaggy dog at her side. She still held the small, recurve bow of the Huntress. *I owe you my life. Who are you?* Cillian stayed on the masthead, straining to see more, but the fog swallowed her.

Twenty-seven—Sloane and Chullain

The *Caoimhe* sailed through the night with the helm tied, going where the wind blew them. All on board slept. Their first real sleep since they left the island.

The next morning the sun chased the chill of the night, shrieking seabirds soared, the sea was calm, and the northerly was pushing them they knew not where. It was quiet on the *Caoimhe,* both with thoughts they did not want to share.

Sloane went forward and filled a bucket with seawater. She shrugged out of her tunic and shift and scrubbed herself pink. She then rinsed her clothes and put them back on wet. Glancing aft to the helm, she sent an innocent smile Merle's way. Sloane did not yet know the full power of her beauty and the effect it had on men. She thought no more of the everyday things of life than if she was still amongst the women of the Island.

As she walked aft to join Merle, she heard his thoughts. *She doesn't know what she does to me when she does things like that.*

She sat beside him. "Does it bother you to see me bathe?"

"N . . . n . . . no," he stammered, not looking at her.

"Look at me, Merle. I heard you say I don't know what I do to you when I do things like that. What does that mean?" She laid her hand on his knee.

Merle looked at her hand, and then into her eyes; he picked her hand off his knee and put it in her lap. "I never said anything. You read my thoughts, you do this all the time."

"Oh, Merle, I didn't know this was happening! You mean too much to me."

"But not enough, Sloane. Not enough." Merle would not look at Sloane; he became engrossed in a course change, the rigging and the clouds. "When we make landfall, I am not going with you. I am not part of your destiny."

Sloane knew there were no more words, so she touched his cheek softly before leaving him alone. She went forward and sat, letting the wind finish drying clothes and hair. She did not look back at Merle, although she felt his sadness, and the hurt in his heart. There was nothing she could do, so she willed herself not to hear his thoughts.

Twenty-eight—Shrines

They sailed two nights and one full day. On the second morning, they made the shoreline and followed the seabirds in. They worked together lowering the sail; they had become a good sailing team and enjoyed working with each other. When all was secure and there was nothing left to do except leave, the smiles faded and the silence became uncomfortable.

"I can go part-way with you, to make sure . . ."

"No, Merle, you have done all—. I shall miss you." Sloane gave him a quick hug and a kiss. "You will be a great man one day if you never forget what you have learned on the Island."

"I will never forget you. You have part of my heart." Merle stood, still hoping something would change. He had brushed his hair, spot-cleaned his tunic, and he had even cleaned his fingernails. "Can I be great when I am not whole?"

"Oh, Merle, you mean so much to me." Sloane kissed her two fingertips and laid them on Merle's lips. Then she and Chullain walked across the sandy beach and disappeared into the forest.

Just inside the tree line, she fell to the ground as silent sobs shook her. Chullain nuzzled her, whining with her, until she put both arms around him and rocked until she saw the *Caoimhe's* sail disappear over the horizon.

"It's just us now, boy. Which way do we go?"

Chullain stood, floppy ears perked as much as floppy ears will perk, his nose wet, and quivering as he sampled the air. He took three steps and disappeared behind a giant fern.

"Wait, Chullain. Wait." A moment of panic seized Sloane when her dog disappeared, and she rushed through the ferns. "There you are," she said when she found him sitting in the center of a narrow forest path.

Sloane dropped down and hugged her friend again. "Don't leave me like that again. I never realized how much I needed you until you disappeared." Chullain wiggled with delight at the attention and lathered her face with kisses.

"Well, Chullain of the male intellect, which way do we go?" Sloane asked, facing one way then the other.

"Stay off the path. Follow the rabbit trail. It will lead you to your destination." A rumbly throaty voice came from the shadows of a yew thicket.

"Show yourself so I may see who gives me directions," Sloane said, and she turned slowly to face the voice. She felt no fear. Chullain was not alarmed. But she did feel a little apprehensive.

One large shadow separated from the other shadows and a tall man, whether he was mortal or not Sloane could not determine, stepped onto the trail. From where he stood he remained partially concealed. Sloane could see he was wearing the skins of animals, and his head was adorned with the antlers of a stag.

Sloane felt no danger; Chullain just stood, watching the apparition. "What do I call you, sir, for you to give me directions."

The voice soft but deep, like the grunt of a stag, floated in the air. "I am Hurd the Hunter. This is my forest; the animals of the forest are under my protection. There was harmony when the Sisterhood administered from the Grove Shrine. You and your dog are welcome."

"Hurd, are you mortal?" Sloane asked. A cloud floated across the sun and the forest trail became a room of shifting light and spectral shapes. When the sun again filtered through the forest canopy, Sloane and Chullain were alone.

Chullain snuffled over to the little opening that only a hunter would recognize as a rabbit trail. He looked back at Sloane and pushed into the green growth. Sloane followed, pushing large ferns aside as she went. "This is not so bad, I think we are coming to a clearing." She spoke to Chullain as she walked.

"This is a pretty place." Butterflies were floating through bright lances of sunlight shafting into the many hues of green and brown. Raucous jays were trying to control the airways, and squirrels could be heard scurrying through the trees and leaves.

"Let's sit, boy," Sloane said. "Over there, by the spring." They walked across the opening in the forest. "This is one of the places. Look."

The water bubbled out of a fissure from the face of granite monolith so overgrown it looked like part of the green forest growth. A vine and moss covered sheer wall, part of something ancient.

Peace emanated, and surrounded them. The leaves rustled as if whispering, the water rolled and fell against the rock with a gentle murmur. The smell of fern and mint blended in with the warm comforting odor of old wood filled their senses. Although Sloane did not see the pointy little blue-etched brownish faces at the edges of the grove, she felt their presence. She also detected the movement of a stag as Hurd slipped deeper into his forest.

"This is where we start," she announced to Chullain. Sloane removed the harp from her bag, and sat in the sunlight and butterflies, the first chord of the strings and time stood still.

Twenty-nine—The Warren

The Faerie world, which had not opened to this area in years, opened its portals to the magical notes of Sloane's harp. The Forest Orkneys, the small sharp-featured people who lived secretive lives in the forest, began to gather. All except for one, she slipped off. This Orkney knew where an outsider female lived.

Before she reached the hut, she met the woman coming down the path. "I hear. Has she come?" the worn, but serene matron asked.

The trilling tongue of the forest people answered her, "Speak to me in my tongue, Raave."

"Yes, it is she, and she has a great animal with her." Raave grasped the woman's hand. "Come, Maune, we must hurry."

"No. Now that I know she is here, I will go and find as many of the Sisterhood as I can." Maune turned and walked the way she had come. "The women will gather as of old, on the evening of the third night," she said over her shoulder.

Raave had become fast friends with Maune in the years after the Skirniri had destroyed the Shrine. All Maune would talk about was when the Goddess would send the Seeker to reestablish their Shrine and Sisterhood. Now it happens and she will not even come to the Grove and see. Raave's little blue-etched face showed her disappointment. She would never understand these outsiders.

Sloane played and the music soothed and blended together all who heard it. The Orkney people remained hidden, enjoying the magic of the harp. The Faerie world listened, but now was not yet the time.

When the magic of peace and harmony had stilled and lulled the afternoon to the shadows of evening, Sloane returned the harp to its bag.

"Time to find a place to sleep, Chullain." She had seen the Orkneys and knew how shy they were. She could hear the birdlike little voices, a language she knew from her childhood.

It had been several years since she had heard or spoken it, but she said, "Come out, we are friends," in the birdlike language.

The ferns and myrtles parted, and Raave stepped out. For a moment, she venomously looked back at the males who had pushed her out. Then she turned back and smiled at Sloane. She shyly inched forward, avoiding Chullain.

"Mistress, you may share our food, and take shelter with us against the night chill. Follow me." Raave would not get within touching distance of either Sloane or Chullain.

"What are you called?" Sloane asked.

"I am Raave, daughter of Raave, and daughter of Raave, for seven Raaves, I lead this Warren of Orkneys." Raave announced her lineage and authority with pride.

"I am Sloane—"

Raave raised a little hand and said, "We know you, and why you are here. Come." She turned, entering the Forest.

Sloane bent at the waist and entered a deer path; Chullain's wagging tail disappeared with them in the wall of greenery. The trail was a green tunnel, with intersecting trails crossing at all angles at different places. When they reached a spot under a large oak, Sloane stopped and stood upright. She refused to go any farther. She felt lost; the path had already taken so many turns.

The area was different than the forest they had just walked through, but this was not discernible at first. If you looked closely, you could see multiple paths crisscrossing faintly. There were also domed mounds at irregular intervals. As she watched Sloane saw a child scamper out of one and run to Raave, who scooped the little brown body up with trilling laughter tinkling through the Warren. All the domes had cleverly concealed doors, which were now opening, and whole families were shyly gathering around.

The family groups looked much like the other. All of spear-bearing or child-bearing years had the intricate facial tattoos of each family line. The children ran between family groups receiving hugs or little admonishments, whichever they needed. The men stood, leaning on thrusting spears that came to Sloane's waist in length. It was evident this was a matriarchal society as the men stood in a protective role and the women were in authority in speech and actions.

The whole Warren of Orkneys ate in the open, sitting on the ground around Sloane and Chullain. When Chullain let one of the little Orkneys pull his tail, they accepted him as friendly. They had delighted in feeding the big dog. He had eaten so much he was dozing, with little pointy-faced children climbing all over and sliding down him.

These were possibly the last of this mysterious race. They were larger than leprechauns. They were more mortal than faeries. They did not have the magic of the faerie world. They were closer to Nature than the rest of the humans, The Outsiders, as The Orkneys called them. Raave told their story to Sloane. All present listened as if this was the first time they had heard it.

Thirty—The Story of the Orkneys

Raave was a master storyteller, acting out scenes, assuming many roles. In the beginning they, The Orkneys, ruled this land and there were no outsiders. Living was good; the primal forest went on forever and supplied them with all they needed.

Then one day from the south, The Outsiders appeared. They chopped the trees, cut great trails through the woods. Their great-horned beasts pulled large baskets of everything everywhere, their great hooves destroying homes and gardens, scaring small game. The Orkneys tried friendship and were killed, their belongings stolen, or they were enslaved to work the land of the smelly Outsiders. The Orkneys fought and were driven from place to place deeper into the forest. They grew fewer and fewer.

Raave's small face with the intricate swirls and magical symbols streamed tears as she recounted the great massacre of her people by the large blonde and red-haired men and women. Yes, even women and children joined in killing. After all, the Orkneys weren't human. They were rodent people.

"We came to this place after the Red and Black men killed the women of the Grove," Raave said. "We were accepted by the Gentle Outsider Women. We shared healing knowledge and other magic."

The sun was gone and the moon was in the shadowed condition, indicating this was the first night. Sloane covered her mouth in a little yawn. The sleeping youngsters were carried gently by their parents, and they filed by Sloane with shy little smiles and sometimes feathery touches.

"We will make you a sleeping pallet here. You will not fit in our hutches," Raave said as she spread quilts under the Oak. "You are not a large outsider; you require only four quilts."

"Thank you, Raave. You are a friend."

"I will sleep here with you," Raave announced.

"No, you have your children who need you. Chullain will keep me company. Now go to your children." Sloane turned the little woman around and gently pushed her towards her hutch.

Thirty-one—Living in the Warren

Sloane lay back listening to the night forest sounds, watching the wispy clouds trail across the moon. She let the night consume her. She could feel Chullain breathing, and his tail and leg occasionally twitched against her. So much had happened. Merle and the *Caoimhe* were somewhere out on the same sea as Cillian. Cillian . . . the name meant War and Strife. Sloane knew this, but that is all she knew about the youth in her visions and dreams.

Even now she could see him, as he was when last she saw him, high in the masthead straining to catch a glimpse of them as they sailed into the fogbank. *I hope they have a healer in his long boat,* she thought. He had many wounds. *What is this man to me? What will he be to me?* Sloane felt the liquid belly warmth of the new woman she had become as sleep and dreams claimed her.

A jay announced morning to the forest. The jays, then the crows, added their good mornings to the scratching of squirrels in the trees as the blackness lightened to gray. The chill caused Sloane to snuggle back under the quilts. Once under them she peeked out and saw two sets of merry little eyes shining back at her. Raave's little boy and one other, she didn't know if it was boy or girl. They were giggling softly and whispering to each other.

She didn't want to, but she shrugged off the blankets and stretched, watching the Orkney children out of the corner of her eye. They tittered and pointed. They had virtually no clothes, but the chill air did not bother them. Sloane noticed the other child was female.

"Tasso, Raave, leave our guest alone." Raave the mother materialized out of the domed entrance. "Raave, show our guest where she can take care of morning things."

"Thank you," Sloane said.

She reached down and picked up little Raave. "Tell me where to go. I have a great urgency," she whispered to the little girl, who giggled, and smiled and put her little arms around Sloane's neck, nuzzling up along her cheek. The little girl was covered with fine silky fuzz; that was why she didn't feel the chill. Sloane felt love for these peculiar little people; she hugged, nuzzled, and kissed little Raave. It was a comfort for both of them.

When they came back refreshed to the Warren, Sloane handed Raave to her mother. "How many Raaves are amongst the living?" She asked.

"Just me and my daughter. In five years time, her body hair disappears and she will get the magic symbols that I wear put on her face and body. Come, we eat the morning meal." Raave led Sloane to where Chullain was already gobbling from a pile on the ground.

The Orkneys ate communally. The table was actually a series of tables, end to end. Each family brought a table. The Orkneys no matter the age or status had the same bowl, a pointed spoon used for sticking and holding food, and for carrying liquids to their mouths.

Sloane sat with Raave's family and used a guest bowl. The food looked like pieces of a sponge that Sloane had once seen. Merle had brought it from the sea when he was fishing. There were also white finger-long objects that crunched and tasted slightly tart. The brownish sponge objects were chewy with the consistency of fish and tasted earthy but good.

"What is this we are eating?" Sloane asked. "It is not meat?"

Raave smiled that felinelike smile, her tongue even

appeared in one corner of her mouth, the blue swirls on her cheeks blended and belonged on her face. "No, it is not meat. It grows under the earth. We call it Bakavi. It means, 'no-blood meat.' We eat meat only when we make sacrifice."

During the morning meal, Raave promised help from the Warren in restoring the Grove. Mainly they would be a warning system if the Skirniri again threatened.

"The priestesses who escaped will assemble in the Grove in two nights. Maune will bring those who survived," Raave said.

"Maune? Who is Maune?"

"Maune is a priestess who escaped the Skirniri. She lives close by and tends the grove as best she can. We are friends," Raave said.

"Who is Hurd?" Sloane asked, suddenly remembering the man from the forest. "I met him. He gave me directions to the Grove."

Raave's eyes widened. "He let you see him?"

"Yes, he appeared as a man with antlers for a headdress."

"He is the spirit of Forest and Animals. He watches over us the best he can. To wantonly kill any living thing of the forest, or cut down trees weakens him. He is still weak from the Skirniri raid." Raave placed both her hands in Sloane's. "You are the Seeker. The one who will heal us. This is so if Hurd allowed you to see him."

Sloane laughed. "I am Sloane. I have been a woman but two cycles. I will help rebuild the Shrine and move on. I am only a woman."

She pulled the little Leader of the Warren to her and hugged her. "We will always be friends, Raave. Now show me how to return to the Grove, I have much to do."

Already she was listing the things in her mind that

she had to do. The Shrine Altar and Stone Circle must be rebuilt; sacred fire and water source must be found, purified and blessed. *So much to do.*

Thirty-two—Grove Shrine and Hurd

It was middle morning when they returned to the Grove Shrine. Sloane searched out anything that might have missed destruction. All Shrines were not the same; they were as varied as the women who built them and the land that held them.

She found a circle of thirty-three stones. There was nothing outwardly different about these stones, except all were of uniform size and height.

They were just right for a woman to kneel by or sit on. Some of the stones had been tipped over, all overgrown with creepers, and vines. In the center of these stones was a fire pit and what was once a circular table or altar. The altar top, a slate-gray bottomed round slab, whose top was burnished black, slick and very shiny, had been shoved off and leaned against one of the rough-hewn stone legs. This circular area was not small, and it was not large either. From one side to the other, a person's features could be seen, but one step behind the stone circle and they disappeared. This circle was most powerful when thirty-three women sat or kneeled at their stones. The fire pit was not blackened by smoke, nor did it contain ashes. This was sacred fire, but for now, it was gone. The bronze tripod legs that supported the sacred water vessel were scattered. The shallow-rimmed vessel lay battered and dented in the bottom of the fire pit.

"This is a job? What are you going to do to help? Offer

me some of that precious male logic." Sloane was sweat soaked, her arms and legs showing the scratches of the battle with the creepers. She had tied her hair up with a bandana, but tendrils escaped and hung wetly against her cheeks. Chullain, the object of her conversation, lay in the shade one eye half-open, tail switching when she talked but stopping when she did.

The great red ball of the sun, its heat softened by the approaching night started to slip behind the trees. Sloane surveyed her work. All thirty-three stones were clean, and all but two were upright. The table altar was cleaned but still did not have the burnished stone top set in place. "I don't know how I will get that back in place." She fretted.

She became aware of another presence. She breathed in the essence as it passed. The smell was of rich fresh-turned earth and wet hair. It was not unpleasant.

Hurd materialized and stepped to the huge flat stone. He dropped down, grasped the down side, and slowly stood, legs quivering with the effort; the stone slid up over the boulder leg then thumped in place, with a puff of rock dust in the last lancing rays of the sun.

Hurd looked at Sloane, who was standing disheveled and dirty. "Do you have food?"

Sloane sadly shook her head no. "Sorry. I have nothing to offer you."

Hurd brushed the top of the stone he had just set in place. Where his hand passed, bread, cheese and water appeared. He gestured with his hand, an invitation to eat.

"No. I mean, not yet. I must clean up. I am not fit to sit at a table." She was flustered, and this did not happen to Sloane.

"There is a pool, I will show you. The food will wait." Hurd walked to her, a frightening image. He appeared human and very male. He was tall already, but the stag horns made him seem a giant. He was clad in skins that molded to him like they were his skin. His muscles moved and rippled like a well-cared-for warhorse. There was the musk that Sloane smelled earlier, it emanated from him in waves. His eyes were golden yellow, his skin appeared walnut-hued, and what could be seen of his hair was the color of heart blood.

"Are you mortal?" Sloane asked. She was almost afraid, but drawn too. It was titillating, warm, not unpleasant, and indefinable.

"I can die. Are you afraid of me?" His voice deep, like it struggled to form the words rumbled the airwaves to her.

"No. I am uncertain with you.—Where is this pool?" They had been walking in the darkening forest. Before Hurd the way was clear and the path illuminated as if Sloane was seeing it through Hurd's eyes.

"There." The word was almost the grunt of the stag.

Thirty-three—Hurd's Pool

The now-brightening moon silvered the small pool as if it were a mirror. Sloane reached over her head to slip off her tunic. She stopped and looked to tell Hurd she wanted privacy, but all she saw was the antlers disappear in to the darkness. The musky smell remained.

She was beautiful. Hurd watched from the blackness of the night, his yellow eyes glowing green. Sloane hung her tunic on a branch and stepped into the pool. A double image of her could be seen in the glowing green coals in the darkness.

The water was warm and silky, and the bottom was solid not muddy. Sloane wiggled her toes to make sure the bottom was solid. Then she gracefully sank into the breast deep water. She looked into the darkness. She was sure she heard a muffled snort, and a foot pawing the ground like a buck in rut. She ducked completely under the water soaking her hair. The water lathered when she wanted to wash, and it rinsed the lather out when she wanted it to. *Magic water.* She lay back luxuriating. She felt relaxed, at peace. *Hurd is watching,* she thought. "You mean me no harm, do you?" she said to the darkness.

The green-glowing coals flickered, "No," rolled out of the darkness deep and moving. Then Sloane heard the slight sound of movement, and the green coals flicked out.

The water lulled Sloane into a transcendental sleep. She felt herself float free of her body. She rose above the trees into the darkness of the night. She looked once at the pool, and she saw the form of herself in light sleep. The world below was formless black, except for where the moon glinted off the rivers flowing to the sea. She rose higher, above the stringy clouds, the moon bloomed larger, the stars stood in glittering contrast to the black void, and the silence was overwhelming.

Then in a flashing swoop, she swept out over the North Sea, the clouds and stars and the shiny wave crests, blurred by the swiftness of her passage. The mountains of a land mass slowed her passage through time and space; she flowed into a jagged, rocky entrance to a fjord.

She floated, but with direction. She was being taken somewhere. There were three long boats beached on the rocky shore. A huge fire roared, flickered, and snapped, sending sparks high into the air. Norse warriors were lying scattered, some staggering drunk over the beach.

Some of those who were lying so still, Sloane could tell were dead, and from great gaping wounds.

Away from the fire, the dying and the drunks, a young raider was grimacing as a small clericlike man stitched up his wounds. "Quit your whimpering, Cillian, these are nothing."

Sloane even in her altered state felt her heart pick up a beat, and blood warmed her face and breasts. She floated in close; this was why she was here, this Cillian.

"Go, Balder. Use your healing skills on old Snorri. Leave me to the drinking horn. Come back when I have finished." Cillian roughly pushed Balder away and drank deeply from the horn, mead spilling out over his chin and chest.

Balder shook his head, picked up his healing bag, and went to the nearest body, a cursory examination, then he moved on until he found one that lived.

Sloane settled slowly until she stood in front of the Raider Cillian. Cillian, wiping his chin focused in on the shadowy, opaque, shimmering figure standing in the flickering shadows cast by the roaring fire. "Who are you? Are you shade?" Cillian demanded. "I don't fear you. I am Cillian the Raider. I have just killed Dordar the Sorcerer and his great Bird Slazoo," he boasted, his head held high and his face defiant.

"You great braggart! I helped you!" Sloane's voice penetrated his pain and alcohol-numbed brain. The voice had a harsh edge. It was the way he imagined the ginger-haired one would sound.

"UUNNGGH," Cillian grunted, sucking in his breath, causing the dagger slash across his ribs to open and start bleeding again. He leaned forward, trying to get a better look. To accommodate him, Sloane stepped closer as a cloud uncovered the moon, and for an instant she was visible in all her naked glory.

"Who are you?" Cillian was sober now. "Are you real?" He was bleeding from leg and rib cut now as he reached for her. She was gone.

Sloane instantly found herself back in the pool. She emerged and dressed, and as she did, she noticed all cuts from the creepers were healed. She felt good. She took two steps back the way she came, and the pool vanished. She found herself at the stone table.

Hurd was gone but the food was still there. Sloane sat and ate, not noticing what she ate. *Why is Cillian in my life?* she thought. *No, he is not in my life, only on the edge. But why?*

She didn't notice that when she got up from the table the food and leftovers disappeared. She entered the small tent without wondering where it came from; her mind was on Cillian. She slept that night and dreamed of the Young Raider.

On the rocky beach, Cillian slept fitfully, wounds still weeping red, and the red-haired Sloane in his dreams. She was occupying his very core now.

In the forest grove, Hurd watched the tent where Sloane slept. His eyes hooded with sleep but still watching, opening wide as if looking through the tent walls, then closing to a green glint. He stood blending into the forest like a great stag.

Morning came as all mornings in this part of the world; the sun pinked the horizon far sooner if you were on the beach. If you were in the forest, the trees woke first, since they caught the first rays of the life-giver. The trees then gently woke the jays, who roused everybody else to the morning. As the sun rose and the shadows moved away, the scratching needles and leaves rustling sang good morning as the forest creatures large and small started their day.

Sloane stepped from the tent and stretched smiling. "Thank you, Mother. Thank you for this morning and this place." This was her morning song and prayer.

When she turned the tent was gone, but the table altar was again laden with food. Hurd stepped from the trees, and Sloane joined him at the table. In the morning sun, Hurd's eyes were again golden yellow. The musky and strangely attractive odor wafted on the morning breeze.

"You are not eating?" Sloane asked.

"I ate earlier," he answered. "The women of this grove will be arriving soon, and I will not be seen anymore—"

"Why? This your forest, you must help," Sloane said.

"I have already helped. I can do no more. I must leave." Hurd was facing Sloane as he talked. He seemed a man, but there was a raw primal force behind those golden eyes. It was not cool enough yet, but his breath was visible, like a stag's on a cold winter morning.

Sloane could not hear his thoughts completely, only bits and pieces, but the rutting message she got colored her cheeks. "Yes, you must go," she said. "Only please don't go far."

Hurd stepped from the table and slipped into the trees. As Sloane watched him enter, she saw a giant stag where the trees thinned, he trumpeted loudly and disappeared into the deep forest.

Thirty-four—The Sisters of the Grove

Sloane suddenly felt heavy with a great burden, and all alone. She sat by the bubbling spring. "Go away, Chullain, leave me." And the girl-woman prayed for strength and wisdom. "Help me, guide me," she prayed.

The sun warmed the rock, and the gurgling water comforted her. She then felt peace. "We can do this," she said softly, with great resolve.

"Yes, we can, my dear. Yes, we can."

"I'm sorry, I was praying. I didn't see you arrive," Sloane said to the worn but regal woman who knelt behind her in attitude of mediation. "Are you Maune?"

"Yes, and you are the Seeker, Sloane." Maune stood, but with some difficulty.

"Here. Let me help you," Sloane said, rushing to her side.

"What will I do when you are not around?" Maune asked. She had a gentle gracious smile. She held out her arms, and Sloane stepped into the welcoming motherly embrace.

"Come let us make some tea. There will be more women coming," Maune said. She led Sloane to a cooking area that Sloane had yet to discover.

"I did not know this was here. I did not look behind the ferns," Sloane said.

"This is special fire. Watch." Maune picked up three small logs and set them carefully, together forming a triangle on the firestone. As Sloane watched the logs started to glow, then burst into a hot flame, with no sparks and no smoke.

Sloane grinned at Maune and hugged her again. Then Maune showed her where she had hidden some things to make living pleasant. Soon the aroma of herb tea permeated the grove.

"It smells like we arrived just in time for tea."

"Is that you, Edana?" Maune asked. She stood up to see better.

"Yes, Bevin, Aghna, and Norra are with me. Is that tea ready? We brought bread and cheese."

It was like a picnic. A planning picnic. The six women talked and planned the way women do. Chullain listened for a while, then snorted and walked off to lie down in the sun, occasionally opening one lazy eye at the group.

Maune led with great skill and patience as Edana of fiery temper and size continually interrupted her. The very soft-spoken, gentle, and pale Aghna would quietly put her hand on Edana's arm and her strength soothed Edana's agitation.

Bevin, seemingly unconcerned about what was happening, was singing and humming with a vacant smile but nothing slipped past her.

Norra, tall and willowy, older and wiser in the ways of the sisterhood, always had an answer when Maune her friend looked to her for added wisdom.

Sloane sat with the women, marveling at their beauty and talents, wondering what she had to contribute to this group. Why had the Goddess selected her? What was she going to do?

During the day more women filtered in until there were thirteen. Some had their families with them. The men and children were given another area to stay during the Third Moon Ceremony. Some of the men prepared shelter for their families, while the oldest of the girl children watched the youngsters. These were men of the old religion, and helped their daughters watching the children. They also prepared the meals while their wives were at the ceremony.

Sloane did not know this ceremony; it was a ceremony of this grove only. She stayed on the sidelines, playing the harp as Maune and Norra directed and administered the rites.

The women were now dressed in flowing white robes; special flowers were woven into their hair. They carried long white tapers that glowed with the magic fire. The fire in front of the altar cast a light that did not flicker, did not smoke, and smelled of the flower that bloomed only in the ninth month and third quarter of the third moon. These were the flowers the women had in their hair. They filed in from the oldest to the youngest. They seemed to float; their faces were serenely peaceful as they sang.

O Earth Mother!
We praise Thee:
that seed springs forth,
that flower opens,
that grass waves.
We praise Thee:
for winds that whisper
through the shining birch,
through the lively pine,
through the mighty oak. We praise Thee,
for all things, O Earth Mother,
Who givest Life!

They moved around the circle of stones, where they stopped in front of every other one. So the circle of thirty-three stones would be complete.

The fire in the pit dimmed, the tapers faded, the plaintive chords of Sloane's harp filled the Grove with reverence felt by everyone. For this moment there was peace and harmony in a three-league area.

Women, who had been hesitant to come on Maune's invitation, left the farm, the bed, whatever they were doing, and started the journey to the Grove.

The Sisterhood sang:

> We all come from the Goddess,
> and to her we have returned:
> As our ancestors worshiped her,
> air, land, and sea.
> Hoof and horn, hoof and horn,
> all that dies shall be reborn.
> Corn and grain, corn and grain,
> all that falls shall rise again.

As the ceremony drew to a close, the women joined hands and, taking gliding steps, they moved their circle to their right. Each woman paused in the position occupied by the woman to her right. At each pause they felt all the hurts and all the joys of their sister. When the circle finally made a complete turn and the sisters were standing where they started, they were one in complete harmony with each other and all that they touched in their lives. They stood the circle unbroken; hands clasped, their eyes still dreamy, and then there was the faint cry of a newborn. The women looked at each other, disengaging their hands they swiftly went to their families.

The ceremony was over, and a peaceful night reigned. From the depths of the forest, Hurd's eyes, green in the dark, watched, blinked and watched.

Sloane stayed the winter. She lived with Maune. And Maune, like Idun and Gwen before, taught Sloane the mysteries of life and the art of being female in a male-dominated world. In return Sloane taught the healing art to those women who had the gift. In the evenings she and Bevin also taught the magic of music to all who wanted to learn. But most of all Sloane learned about family life in the world. She saw the interaction of wife and husband in good marriages, struggling marriages, and bad marriages.

"Why would I want to tie myself to one man? Why would I want to clean up after him and three or four children?" she asked Maune one quiet winter evening in front of the blazing hearth.

"You might not want that for a life. The life of a woman who mothers is not easy. But the rewards sometimes make it worthwhile. You are a woman. You may be one who can direct her future. Most of us can't. We take what we get and make the best of it." Maune spoke to the fire and to the ghosts of her past. Sloane listened with them.

The day the wind was again from the south and the storks returned from their African migration, Sloane announced it was time to resume her commission from the Goddess.

Thirty-five—North

"Where will you go?" Maune asked. "There is no need to leave. We have much work yet to do."

"You have all the stones filled. You are thirty-three now, thirty-three sisters of the Grove. They will do what needs to be done," Sloane said. "Hurd is stronger now. The circle of protection is there."

She said good-bye to Maune in the Grove, but she

stopped at the Warren and said good-bye to Raave and all the Orkneys. As she said her farewells, the golden yellow eyes of Hurd watched. He had had no further contact with Sloane other than watching, and watching.

Sloane and Chullain left the woods behind and started the walk north along the coastline. Suddenly Sloane stopped, and turned full around, facing the dark silent forest. She lifted her right hand. From the trees came the mighty trumpeting call of the Forest Stag. "Good-bye, Hurd of the Forest," she said. The trumpeting call answered her but gradually faded to the sound of the wind and the gulls screeching overhead.

"Where we going now, boy? Does that great male brain of yours have any ideas?" she asked her dog companion.

Chullain looked up at her, his large pink tongue lolling out of his mouth. "Whuufff," he said.

Sloane's laughter rang out as she dropped down on her knees and hugged her faithful friend.

They walked a rugged goat path along the cliffs that faced the sea. The path had not been used for a long time. The drop was sheer down to the jagged jumble the sea was crashing on; the seas were always high and heavy at this spot. The path dropped to almost sea level with the sheer rock wall, against one shoulder and the sea spray air of the fall to the rocks against the other. The sea birds, gulls, and terns nesting in these cliffs protested noisily at their passage. The lower path was even more perilous; the rock trail was slippery from the spray and sea slime that coated parts of the narrow path.

"Ugh, I want a bath as soon as we get to a beach area," Sloane said after she fell slipping to one knee. Her legs and shift were covered with the greenish oily-textured moss.

Chullain for all his bulk was bounding from rock to rock, intent on knocking one of the shrieking, flying pests out of the air. His coat too was matted with all the nastiness of their passage along the rock face. He stopped on a ledge above Sloane, with a woeful look of defeat.

Sloane had to steady herself, her laughter coming hard and fast, joyously bounding off the rocks and out over the sea.

*   *   *

Far, far away to the north, a Norseman was looking out over the cold gray sea. He thought he heard faint laughter. He was sure his ginger-haired dream was real. He remembered her as he last saw her. He knew not love or how to love. His only experiences had been war and strife. When her face came to him in a dream, he felt a softness that was foreign to his emotions. The laugher faded to the slapping of the sea against the rocks, and her face slid to that secret place he did not know he had within. He felt alone.

*   *   *

Sloane crawled over a boulder that had fallen and blocked the path. When her head cleared the top, she saw a clear, black-sand beach ahead.

"Come on, boy. Bath time." She jumped down on the smaller rocks as nimble as the goats that use the trail. She dropped her shoulder bag first, and then threw off tunic and shift. Her bare legs flashed white as she ran across the stretch of beach. When she hit the water, she fell forward in a running surface dive that carried well out in the sound. She stood like a daughter of the sea in innocent beauty, her laughter bouncing off the rocks and dying here. Sloane swam out to where the breakers were throwing up great crashing waves, and circling, she swam back to the beach. The water was cold and when she left the water, her skin was dimpled with the chill bumps. Her chin quivered, wanting to chatter, but she clenched her jaw. Sloane retrieved her bag and removed soap for her hair; she sat on rock at the water's edge and completed her bathing.

She sat with the sun slowly warming her body, the chill bumps disappeared, and her hair dried. Chullain lay nearby, his great coat still wet and tangled. He looked up at her with his sad soulful eyes.

"Come here. Let me get the tangles out," she said.

They sat with the sea lapping the rocks, Sloane combing the tangles out with her fingers, and Chullain's tail thumping contently. They both thoroughly enjoyed each other.

Sloane wondered what it would be like to love a man, a man like the Raider, Cillian. Chullain wondered what they were going to eat and when.

The night was coming on hard and fast and cold. Sloane was hurriedly digging shellfish, and she happened to see an opening in the cliff face. When she climbed up to it, she found a small cave that had been lived in before. She gathered driftwood for a fire and with firerock and knife blade, she made a fire.

She fished a mussel off the hot coals. "Thank you, Merle, wherever you are. From you I learned or I would have gone hungry this night. Goddess, thank you for Merle and the mussels."

Sloane and Chullain watched the water of the cove whipped into a savage fury by the wind. The wave tops were silver with an eerie glow. It was the only light in the cove, as the stars and moon were blanketed. But the little fire just back from the cave mouth winked cheerfully in the heartless black night.

The walls and ceilings of the cave told the story of previous inhabitants. Sloane made a small torch and explored her home for the night. The flicking light revealed handprints at different levels on the walls; there were running bison with arrows and spears hanging from them, pursued by stick-figure people. There was a ferocious bear taking up almost all the space from the floor to the ceiling of the cave.

But at the very end of the cave, set in a niche, Sloane found an object that took her breath away. It was a small figure with a protruding stomach and pendulous breasts.

"The cave of the Old Mother," Sloane whispered. "Old Mother, we will be gone in the morning. Thank you for sharing your home with us."

Sloane cleaned the droppings and refuge of small animals from the Old Mother and her niche, then she went back to her fire and she and Chullain slept protected. They were in the Old Mother's home.

Thirty-six—Evil in the Morning

The first rays of the sun lanced into the cave, at first warm and comfortable on her cheek, but then the dust-mote-laden rays moved into her eyes, waking her. The sea breeze was soft and fresh, wafting in through the narrow entrance, bringing with it the barking of seals that must have sought shelter in the cove during the storm.

Sloane made a last inspection and clean-up of the sanctuary of the Old Mother, and then she piled stones in the entrance, closing it. The beach was littered with debris and parts of a ship that had succumbed to the storm. Sloane made her way slowly down the tangle of rocks to the beach. She had also seen what looked to be bodies, scattered amongst the litter of the storm. The birds had not yet discovered the meals, partially buried in the black sand. Sloane did not think any were alive, at least the first one she encountered wasn't.

Sloane didn't know what it was until she saw the ears. Only then did she realize that it was a shaven head, barely visible with the body covered by sand. She didn't stop. She went to the next one that was bobbing in the ebb and flow of the waves. This one had a shaven pate too. His body, though bleached and scoured by water and sand, bore traces of red and black paint.

Skirniri. It had been eight years since she had run from them, but these looked to be Skirniri. The rage that she felt when they killed Gr'ainne roiled through her. She drew back to kick the corpse but stopped. *I won't kick you, but I won't bury you either. The gulls and crabs can have you.*

Sloane walked over to the beached section of the ship. It had broken in half, so she was able to walk into it. The ballast stones, or what was left of them, were spilled in a trail to the ship. There were three other bodies lying with arms intertwined, just inside the hull. They were young boys still with full heads of hair. Sloane had heard of the Skirniri practices and wondered if perhaps the boys were not better off now than if the ship had survived. Chullain, his nose to the decking and bulkheads, sniffed his way around the wreckage. Sloane closed the eyes of one of the boys, said a little prayer for them, and then followed Chullain.

The ship had been a galley of sorts; the cargo she had carried was not evident. Chullain was sitting patiently at the hatch in what was left of the stern section; the two great steering oars had been torn away. Sloane tried the door, it was difficult, but it slowly swung open. She was not prepared for the depravity that greeted her eyes as they adjusted to the darkness.

The only light was from the morning sun slicing the darkness along the opened seams of hull planking. The ship had been stitched together, as was the method of construction, and the storm had stretched the stitching ropes. Great gaps grew between the planks. It was like a great barn from the inside, only the light sluiced sideways instead of up and down.

One slashing ray cut across the slumped visage of the Skirniri Priest ridiculous now in death, as he was terrible in life. Sloane knew that there was never one Skirniri there were always two. So she stood and surveyed the cabin. Sloane knew this black evil when the Skirniri had raided the Forest Shrine when she was four.

She could feel the fine hairs on her arms stiffen; her breathing was short and shallow pants of fear. She willed herself to inhale deep and slow. She forced her thudding heart to return to a slow beat of normalcy.

Chullain had begun a steady growl when the door opened, and now he pushed ahead of Sloane to be between her and any danger. His growl fell to almost a whimper, but ratcheted up to a snarl the likes of which Sloane had never heard. He had bumped into a pile. She stood still straining to see.

The cabin was slowly being illuminated. The sun, climbing towards midday's apex, breached a hatch cover that the storm had blown away. The light flooded onto the bulkhead behind them and spilled across the floor, blinding them both for an instant.

Now the total horror of the room was screaming at

them. Sloane's eyes flew wide open in shock, and then snapped shut with denial. The room revealed a pile of bodies, male, female, both animal, and human—directly in front of them. The Skirniri were evidently trying to appease the storm gods with sacrifice. The bodies had been torn, dismembered, and gutted in a frenzy of killing. Sloane was peeking at the carnage when the movement of a live Skirniri was detected. He was crouching in the corner gnawing on something.

Chullain tensed for the leap. He was coiled, crouching fury. His lips pulled back, revealing large yellowish-white teeth, with blood-red gums. Sloane grabbed the fur at his neck, and he froze, not taking his eyes off the apparition.

It was still dark in the corner, but the Skirniri's eyes shone white. His shaven head reflected the sunlight as he stood. His body retained some of the red and black paint he wore, his mouth was smeared with gore.

Sloane tightened her grip on Chullain, who was quivering, wanting release.

"A woman." The Skirniri stepped fully into view. He dropped an object and drew a short sword.

Sloane looked at the object he had dropped and recognized a mutilated infant. She released Chullain.

Chullain, in a silent leaping attack, struck the Skirniri Priest full in the chest, knocking him down, ripping his throat out. He moved so fast the evil priest had no time to defend himself. Sloane watched as the Skirniri legs twitched their last.

"Come, Chullain," she said. As soon as he heard her command, Chullain stopped ripping the thing up. He walked back, looking at his mistress, not understanding exactly what had happened. His fur was soaked with Skirniri blood, his muzzle still dripped of it.

"Come, Chullain, let's clean you up." Sloane led him out of the wreck and took him to a tide pool. "Good boy, good dog, thank you, Chullain," was her little song, to him as she gently washed him clean.

It was almost early evening before Sloane dragged the four bodies from the beach and put them inside the wreckage.

"Go get more driftwood and bring it here, boy," she said as she stacked it in the ship. It was evening before she was satisfied they had enough. Sloane brought from her bag three of the magic fire sticks. Arranging them in the triangular shape, she started the hot fire.

"Come, boy. We spend another night in Old Mother's home. She will welcome us." As they walked back for the climb up the rocks, the fire behind them rose higher and hotter. Neither dog nor woman looked back.

Thirty-seven—Ma's Spine

Before the first fiery edge of the sun burnt the top of the sea, Sloane and Chullain cleaned the cave and climbed higher, to the ridge back trail heading north. It was a tricky climb, but Chullain went first, with his good eyes picking out the path, and there was an enough moon left low in the western sky to help. Sloane steadily moved upward, her mind blank from all the horror she had just seen. It was cool, but soon she was covered in a sheen of sweat, and it felt good. The air was not tainted with the decaying odor that comes from vegetation at water's edge, or now from the smell of burning wood and flesh. It was good clean mountain air that she pumped into her lungs.

Soon it was light enough that she stopped for her first look around. "Stop, boy. Let me catch my breath."

The beauty of the mountains was so stark and beautiful it was contagious. She felt the driving urge to see what was across the next peak. Straight ahead the path narrowed to a one-person trail, on both sides a sheer drop. "We are walking on Ma's Spine, Chullain."

The spine was treacherous and sparse. The only vegetation was a four-petalled pale red flower on a spindly stem, with one or two leaves of palest green and some brownish-green lichen. The trail seemed to fade to a black, with a bluish shade of white. In the distance a mountain floated with the clouds.

Below on the left side of the spine trail was jumbled jagged rocks and boulders barren and inhospitable until Sloane saw the white-and-brown specks of mountain sheep walking daintily along impossible terrain. At the very end, down at the bottom of the hole, was a flash of water and green. Sloane wondered if there were people there.

Sloane looked back to where they had come from. She looked toward the beach and sea. It was like looking into the open door of the potter's oven. She saw the huge sun gilding, melting the sea into the sky. The beach was fuzzy in the glare, and so she did not see the long boat as it crested the breakers and coasted to a stop at the beach. "Come on, boy, it's light. I can lead now." Sloane adjusted her shoulder bag, and they started their trek north along Ma's Spine.

*   *   *

As the long boat ground upon the shallows, Cillian splashed ashore. They had guided on the fierce fire they had seen all night. Cillian was sailing with Ivar, a chieftain of the farthest frozen north. It was a hard, fierce, and cold place—of land and men.

"What is it? What burned?" Ivar shouted from the Serpent's head, which meant they were warring.

"It was a ship, a galley of sorts. It's nothing but ashes now," Cillian shouted back.

"Archers, alert," Ivar shouted and his warriors took their bows and stations along the shore side of the long boat. "Cillian, search it out. See what you can find."

But Cillian was already looking. He could see the telltale signs of driftwood being dragged to the wreck, and bones could be seen in the ashes. He followed a set of small feet, as they walked to the cliffside access to the hidden cave. All of a sudden, he knew who had made those prints. He had to protect her.

"Nothing, I find nothing," he hollered back to the long boat.

Soon Cillian was at his oar, and the long boat was clearing the breakers and sailing south. He rowed automatically. That was her foot that made that print, she was there. Cillian knew what would have happened to any young woman found by this crew. *Some day, Ginger Hair, you will be mine. Some day.*

Thirty-eight—The Black Man

Now that the sun was low, almost hidden by the mountain range, Sloane noticed the chill. Ma's Spine trail veered to the northeast now. She picked up the pace to keep warm and to make the protection of the rock wall that she could see in the distance. She was sure she had to reach it if she wanted to survive the night. Along the way

83

she picked up any wood or tinder that she could find, stuffing it into her bag, as she did not see any trees up ahead that would furnish firewood.

This situation was life-threatening. Chullain, sensing the emergency, galloped ahead, scaring a herd of mountain goats. They clattered down the mountainside, scattering small rocks in a landside.

Sloane heard Chullain barking rapidly; she knew this to be his calling attention to something. She hitched her bag tighter, and she ran to him. The trail was wider and smoother now, with evidences of animals passing. If the day had been younger and Sloane fresher, she would have seen the patches of graze in the rocks descending into a broad valley. As it was she was numbing fast from the cold, and she was not thinking well.

Up ahead, Chullain was eating something off the ground, his tail wagging furiously as Sloane approached. He looked up, and then went back to chewing and chomping on a chunk of meat. "Where'd you get that, boy?" She was starting to shake, and her teeth were chattering.

"That's part of a great-toothed cat I killed. Come on in, it's good eating."

Sloane could not see the speaker or where she should go.

"Sir, forgive me, but I do not see you? Can you give us shelter?" Sloane was not fearful of the voice. It had to be good. It had fed her dog.

"Hmmm, just a minute. Now you can see me?"

Sloane watched as the rock face began to move, first a booted foot swung out, then the leg, followed by the upper body. The head and the other leg were still embedded within the rock face. The one free arm strained to push against the rock to force the rest of the speaker out.

"Do you require some help?" Sloane asked, her body tremors lessened at this spectacle.

"Uunngghh. No." Out he popped, falling back and catching himself on his hands. "I've got to work on that a little more." The speaker had a merry sort of face, long, with large ears, and huge black eyes. His hair was of tight wool and was close to the skull. His skin was black, the bottom of a well.

"Are you all right?" Sloane asked. She had never seen a black man before.

"Of course, this becoming part of a rock is harder than becoming part of a tree. But it will just take practice." The cheerful black man stood up and threw his arms out to embrace Sloane. "Welcome, Sloane, I have been expecting you."

Sloane did not flinch; she returned the embrace even though she did not know if the man's Black condition was temporary or not. "When does your color become normal? And what are you called?" She asked, stepping back from the embrace.

"I am Nuba. And this is my color.—Come, it is getting chill, you are turning blue and that is not your normal color. Inside it's warm, and we eat long-toothed cat." Nuba guided Sloane off the path and around the large rock face he had just popped out of. He stepped off the little path, turned a sharp corner, and disappeared.

The wind shrieked through the opening in the rocks. Sloane stopped, where did Nuba go? She saw the drop, the emptiness. They were so high. Small wispy clouds floated below them. The wind whipped and tore at her hair and clothes. *If I take two more steps, I will fall to my death, and if I don't, I shall freeze.* "Nuba," she called, the wind blowing it back into her teeth. "Nuba."

"Don't believe your eyes, Sloane. Where could I have gone? Come into Nuba's home." The voice sounded as if it was within reach just over the windblown edge.

Sloane gripped her bag, took one step, then the second, off the sheer drop—and she stepped into a warm, well-lit room. There were no walls, but there were walls; she could see the mountains, the valley far below, but there was no wind. It was quiet. She took a quick look around then looked wonderingly at her host.

"Welcome to my home. The table is set." Nuba took her elbow and guided her to a table like no table she had ever seen. There were plates for two and eating tools that shone like gold. The drinking bowl was of the same hue, but set with red, green, and blue stones. The main course was meat or something that looked like meat but was sliced already. There were bowls of boiled vegetables, white, orange, and green. She did not know what any of the food was.

"It looks good. It has been a long time since I sat down at table; I hope my manners haven't fled. May I warm up and look around first?"

"Of course." The long black face, split by the dazzling smile and flanked by those large ears, might have caused some to laugh. But Sloane saw only a good, kind man with extraordinary powers. She was going to find out everything about this Nuba.

"It's good to get out of the cold," Sloane said, bypassing the table, marveling at the room. The room was as large as she made it. If she walked towards a transparent wall, she never reached it. The furnishings weren't there until you needed them or passed in touching distance of them, and then they were exactly what you wanted, and expected.

Nuba watched Sloane with that knowing smile and gentle expression on his black face that Sloane didn't notice anymore.

"I'm hungry, Sloane, sit and eat with me. I'm sure you have figured out what is happening."

Sloane walked back to the table, still marveling that the large condor that sailed by did not see them. She was walking suspended hundreds of feet above that valley that changed colors from black purples, greenish browns, all interspersed with jagged, jumbled rocks, sometimes small, stunted, misshapen spruce trees. At the very bottom, through wispy clouds, she could see a patch of green, with farms and towns and people stretching eastward.

"Your home is surprising," Sloane said, between bites of whatever the main course was.

"Here, you haven't had any of these," Nuba said, passing her a bowl that gleamed gold and was filled with green shoots of something.

"This is not what it seems. Is it, Nuba?"

"This is a place for you to secure nourishment and warmth or you would have perished," Nuba said. "And it is a lesson in survival."

"This Magic, is it real or am I imagining it?" Sloane asked. As she ate, she had never tasted anything that was so taste-satisfying and fulfilling.

"Am I real? This home, is it real? This meal, is it not real?" Nuba questioned. "Do you not see me, and hear me? Are you not warm, and fed?"

"Yes, now, but I was very cold when I arrived. Maybe I am dead or fainted and this is not real." Sloane leaned forward, closer to Nuba. "I have never seen a black man. How do I know there are such men? This must be a dream."

"Maybe, maybe not? " Nuba said. "I have gifts for you to help you down the mountain. See if these fit." He handed her some leg gaiters of thick reddish fur, and a long coat of the same animal.

Sloane knelt, wrapped the furs around her lower legs and bound them Norse fashion. "They are warm." She slipped her arms into the large coat that Nuba held out for her. Then, like all women, she luxuriated in the warmth and softness.

Nuba, whether real or imagined, was still a man. He felt the tug of admiration tinged with lust. "You are a beautiful mistress. The furs and your hair; you are like a beautiful furred woman."

"Thank you, Nuba. I feel sleepy now. It must be all the food and cold." Sloane felt pretty and tired. She was overwhelmed by a great weariness. Chullain was already asleep in front of the small fire, his rear legs twitching in his sleep, and giving little sleep whhuuffs.

"Sit here, leave your furs on. I'll talk to you before you sleep." From nowhere a large couch appeared and Sloane lay back in it. Nuba, still talking to her, sat on the floor close to her.

"You should go down in to the valley—. A village—. On the coast Norns—." Nuba's voice droned on in her head as Sloane slipped into deep, healing sleep.

Whuufff. Chullain woke first and nudged Sloane as she slept curled up in a niche in the rocks, the small fire flickering feebly, one little strand of smoke rising and dis-integrating. A light sugaring of snow covered the rocks, but Chullain and Sloane had hardly any on them.

Sloane pried herself from the protected spot in the rocks. She stood stretching, her arms thrown wide; her coat and leggings made her look wild, free and very beautiful in the cold morning light.

"Good-bye, Nuba, thank you," she said. "Come on, boy, we go down into the valley."

Chullain was at the ledge looking down and sniffing

all along the trail, up the face of the rock that Nuba popped out of. He looked at Sloane quizzically.

"Confusing, isn't it, boy. It happened but it's time to go."

Thirty-nine—The Valley

The snow scattered like dust in an empty barn each time Sloane's feet padded down. The air was cold in her nose, and she could see each breath she took. After climbing over what looked to be an impassable snarl of rocks, they stepped on a shepherd's trail. *Nuba must have told me about this trail as I slept. We would never have found it from where we were.*

Chullain had picked up the pace, nose to the ground, puffs of steamy breath billowing up around his head. He would sniff there, then go a few paces and sniff again, from one side of the trail to the other.

"What is it, boy? What do you smell?" The walk now was enjoyable; good trail, no sign of traffic yet though Chullain seemed to think something had used it recently.

"Chullain, can you tell if it is a man or a woman you're after? I wish it to be woman. I need to talk to woman again." Sloane's head was full of the happenings of her life, and she wanted an older, wiser woman to talk to.

Chullain was padding along ahead now, not sniffing; Sloane couldn't see his breath any more. The strain on her thighs was less too; The angle of descent was less. The tree line was just ahead as the big rocks had shrunk in size to scattered boulders and rocky ground.

Sloane stopped at one of the last outcrops of rocks

that still merged with the mountain. She knelt and removed her furry leggings; it was warm now and time to return them. Then she took off the coat that Nuba gave her, and she laid the garments on the rocks. Chullain came over and sniffed them, turned and padded down the path towards the trees.

"Thank you, Nuba," she said softly and followed Chullain.

When they reached the trees, Sloane stopped and looked back, and gasped.

A giant reddish long-toothed cat stood in the place of the coat. It switched its tail lazily, then turned majestically and bounded up the rocks back to the high country. Sloane watched as it reached a high point outlined by the glory of the blue sky, it raised its head and roared.

Sloane felt a shiver run through her, and Chullain gave a timid little growl. When they looked back, the cat was gone.

"Good-bye, Nuba. Let's go, boy, we have to find someone to take us in or make a camp soon."

It was pleasant walking through the aspens, the sound of their steps in the leaf-strewn floor, and Chullain's panting was all that Sloane heard. "Where are the birds, boy?"

This was strange; even the trees seemed quieter than they should be. There was hardly any wind rustle at all. Sloane stopped at the tree line; they were at the other edge of the belt of trees. The valley lay open before them. It was already evening where they stood because the mountain hid the sun. But the valley lay in late afternoon sunlight. The greens, and yellows and browns of the squared fields had that strange soft liquid light of a dream. The stone fences that separated the fields stood in sharp relief to the colors contained. She could see four cottages, the white softened to an ivory hue with the trickle of blue-white smoke wafting skyward.

Forty—Raiders

Many leagues to the south, Ivar's Raiders were finishing their raid on the Saxon monastery. Cillian watched as old Snorri went down the line of kneeling priests, grabbing a handful of hair and pulling the head back and opening the throat with his Sumerian short knife. Snorri looked up and saw Cillian watching. He grinned as he pulled the knife across an old priest's throat, "Messy work if they spout on you," he shouted and grabbed the hair of a young novice of ten or so years.

Cillian turned away: this was not war. This was butchery. He wandered in the sanctuary, the entire gold reliquary objects had already been carried off. He heard muttering and he found his old friend Balder the Healer wandering amongst the Sanctuary wreckage.

"This is not right. We are dammed." An oldish man, he picked up a broken crucifix and attempted to put it back together, tears of anguish streaming down his face.

"Balder, it is done. Come, let's go back to the long ship." Cillian took the crucifix, dropped it behind him, and led Balder from the sanctuary. "You can't undo this. You can't even pray about it: you quit praying years ago."

"Cillian, how long are we going to sail with Ivar?"

"Not long.—Old friend, can you dream while you are awake?" Cillian asked.

"Did you see her again?" Balder stepped over the bodies of sheep; the Vikings killed everything that lived at the monastery.

91

"No.—Pick up that lamb. I'll carry these two: we'll eat them tonight.—I think she controls when I see her. I want to see her again." Cillian held the lambs out to drain so he wouldn't get so much blood on his clothes.

Balder watched this, usually Cillian was covered in gore after a fight. "You didn't draw blood?"

"No, I fight warriors, not clerks and priests." Cillian shouldered the lambs and they both headed for the beach.

"I want that woman," he said, more to himself than Balder.

"She may be a witch," Balder said.

"I don't care if she is Inanna herself," Cillian said.

Balder sucked in sharply: he started to make the cross sign, but he stopped it in time. "She is the Sumerian Goddess of Death."

"This woman. I will have her," Cillian said as he flung the lamb carcasses down to be butchered.

Balder skinned the lambs for the fire. He watched Cillian brood. He was worried for his ward; he was becoming obsessed with this woman that only he had seen.

Forty-one—Hole in the Hill

Sloane almost tumbled into an overgrown washout, where once a huge boulder had rested. But hundreds of years ago, melting snow pushed it tumbling into the valley below. She moved the scrub oaks and creepers away, and found a large comfortable recess into the hillside.

"Chullain. We shall make this home for a while. Use your nose see if anyone else will be trying to share with us tonight." Chullain was already sniffing things out. His tail was moving in that excited new place, new smells wag. When he reappeared, he sat down with that foolish tongue hanging-out grin that Sloane loved. "Whuufff."

"Nothing has been here for long time. This is a good place."

"Thank you, Chullain. I was wondering if you were ever going to talk to me again?"

"You have need of male guidance, Sloane. We are new to this hillside and this valley. Tonight is a good night for the Harp to announce us to whomever else is here." This time Chullain's ever-present dangling tongue was in his mouth, as if he was trying to look more dignified.

Sloane scratched his ears. "You are right. Tonight we will play to the parallel worlds. But first we make this more livable."

Inside their new home, which was still really just a large hole in the hillside, Sloane swept out one side near the back wall, which she lined with what leaves and small scrub shin oak that she cut from places on the hillside. She did not want to shout their presence to whomever happened by. So she cut skillfully, and you could not tell that anything had been removed, or that anybody was living there. She built a small fire and made a hot tea to go with the bit of bread and cheese. Sloane gave most of the food to Chullain, who without a thought as to where it came from, gobbled it up and looked for more.

"Sorry, boy, we will get food in the valley tomorrow." She patted his head and gave him her piece of bread. The tea was enough. Chullain swallowed the bread in one gulp, throwing his head back and swallowing, his tail thumping up small dust clouds on the cave floor.

Daylight softened and the shadows lengthened. Sloane sat near the entrance of her temporary home.

She was drinking her second bowl of tea as she

93

watched the sky's blue, lighten to grayish blue, then to gray slashed with orange as the sun hung for an instant above the high hills. Then plummeted the world into darkness, as it dropped below the horizon.

The small fire took away the chill in the air, but the chill of melancholy covered both Sloane and Chullain. There was nothing homey about this hole in the ground. And on an almost empty stomach, it seemed even worse.

"Maybe we should have kept on walking into the valley?" Sloane asked.

"Hhooo, hoo," floated in from the blackness. Chullain sat up, looking at Sloane for direction.

"Relax, boy, it's just an owl." But Sloane felt something other than ease when she comforted Chullain.

Forty-two—Gwen Tells the Story of Mouadas

"Hhhoooo, hhhhhoooo." That might be an owl, but it was unnerving. Sloane took her Celtic Bard's harp from her bag and struck the chords of a lullaby. All the night noises of crickets and other bugs and the small hunters in the weeds stopped. Chullain lay back down and closed his eyes, his breath puffing little dust storms in the dirt floor when he breathed.

The worlds usually in friction with each other began to line up. Portals opened. Sloane played another lullaby, and then she played the Ballad of the Glen Faeries.

Chullain's eyes popped open at the audible sound of a heavy door opening. Light suffused the dirty little hole they were in, and Gwen stepped in.

Sloane dropped her harp, but the music continued.

"Gwen, I wanted you to come, and you're here. Thank you."

Gwen held out her arms and hugged the little girl of twelve. "I felt your need, Sloane. You should have called sooner."

Sloane felt the warmth and love of the Faerie Queen, and she did not want to be the grown-up. But she had to be. Gwen held her, comforting her, and stroking her hair, crooning such as a mother with her child. Then she said, "This residence you picked, was there no other place?"

Sloane couldn't help it. She laughed, until she was out of breath. "Oh, Gwen, I didn't look in the valley. I wanted to find out more before I went there. This is pretty bad, isn't it?"

"Come back with me. The Glen Faeries will welcome you as a queen, which you will be when I go."

"I can't. But I will accept all the help you can give me. I do not know why Nuba wants me to go into the valley."

"Nuba is known to the faeries. He is a wandering wizard. It is said he once lived on the land that sank." Gwen was moving about in the hole they were in. A flick of the hand here, and a sleeping pallet replaced the sticks and leaves. "Why didn't you do this, Sloane?" Another flick and the walls were smoother and harder not crumbling and dropping bugs and dirt on them.

"I don't know why I always do things the hard way. I suppose I will always think as a mortal. Besides, you wouldn't be here if I had used magic. Would you?" Sloane embraced her faerie friend, kissing her cheeks. "Maybe your magic can manifest some biscuits and tea."

Soon they were sitting at a small table in the warm glow of faerie light and friendship warmth.

"Nuba was in the cold mountains because he was driven from the valley by Mouadas," Gwen said, sipping her tea. "I've missed you, Sloane. Even Old Michlean of the glen leprechauns came to see me, wanting news of you."

"I've missed you all too. But I have been too busy to get heartsick over it. What is Mouadas that it drove Nuba out of his valley?" Sloane asked. "Are you going to stay the night?"

"Heavens, no! I am going back to the glen. And you should come with me."

"Gwen, tell me what is Mouadas?"

"Who is Mouadas?" Gwen stood, her brow wrinkled with consternation. "Mouadas is a woman sorcerer. She was once a healer from the place of hot sands and humped animals."

"I never heard of such a place. I have seen sand on the beach, and the great oxen of the farm. Being a healer is good, a healer knows our Goddess," Sloane said, trying to picture what Gwen had just revealed.

"Her home was many leagues to the south. Yes, she once was a priestess. She is not lost yet. She is bitter, hateful, and has no compassion. She has not turned to evil, or the black craft yet. I feel so sorry for her." Gwen's voice quavered with emotion.

"Why? How did Nuba come to be driven out of this valley? Was it his home first?"

Gwen placed her hand on Sloane's across the table, "You are not coming back with me, are you?"

"No. I am called, driven, even compelled. I do not really know why, but I must go into the valley." Sloane grasped Gwen's hand, bringing it to her lips. "Tell me what I need to know."

"Mouadas lived in an oasis village in the great burning sand. She was of the old way and a Priestess of the Goddess. Christian and Saracen lived in harmony; they met to trade for salt and cloth in the oasis town of Sitnala.—Pour me more tea please." Gwen sipped her tea and continued. "Then came the great religious wars. The entire Western Christian world mounted a great crusade to reclaim the holy lands of Jesus. The Saracen raised an opposing army. Sitnala was between them." Gwen paused, collecting her thoughts.

Sloane sat patiently rubbing Chullain's ears. She was hearing things about a world she did not know existed. Sloane felt the excitement of new and strange place building inside her.

"Sitnala was taken by the Christian forces without a fight. But the Christians were not generous victors; anyone who did not believe as they did were treated badly. The Christian soldiers took what they wanted.

"They took Mouadas's home and destroyed her artifacts. Her man was killed defending his family. Mouadas and her children were turned out in the streets." Gwen was feeling every word, and as she spoke them, Sloane was seeing the things as they had happened.

Sloane saw a tall willowy woman veiled and dark. She saw three small children holding on as they stood in a dusty street with heavy cavalry galloping all around them. She saw one child, a girl, fall under the hooves and die. Mouadas could do nothing except hold her other children close and hope the troops would pass.

"She must hate Christians very much," Sloane said.

"Her trials were just starting. The Saracen attacked the Christians at Sitnala. They retook Sitnala and put to the sword all who were not of their faith, or would not convert. Mouadas was raped and beaten, because she would not convert. Her children were taken for slaves." Gwen was crying silent tears now.

Sloane backed out of the visual she had when she saw

the tall dark woman being brutalized by turbaned men. She moved around the table, and both women held on to each other, spreading the horror out between them so they could handle it.

Sloane refilled both bowls with tea. Gwen sipped and started again. "Mouadas recovered, physically but never in mind and spirit. She finally came to this valley embittered against all men, all organized religions. Even the old religion was discarded because the Goddess did not save her children from the slavers."

"That would be hard to accept," Sloane said, remembering when she was four and the Skirniri attacked the grove and the sisterhood, killing many women and her beloved Gr'ainne. Sloane was still not easy about the memory and circumstances. It was good she lived on the Island with the wise gentle women there, to soften the remembrance.

"Mouadas came to this valley alone with only a small hand loom. From this small beginning, she is now the most powerful person in the valley," Gwen said.

"A weaver," Sloane said, even more interested. "How would a weaver of cloth get so powerful?"

"She brought dyes with her. Her small pieces were much sought after because of the vivid colors."

"Where does Nuba enter in this?"

"Nuba raised multi-colored sheep. The wool he sold to locals for making into cloth. The people wanted the different hues of wool to relieve the drabness of their clothing." Gwen paused and yawned.

"Stay the night, Gwen. I must hear the whole story."

"Not here, Sloane. Come, we go to my world." Gwen stood and held out her hand. "The door is still open, two steps and we will be in my home."

Sloane followed Gwen into the soft shimmer of the

second step, and she was in a softer world, a sweeter world. "Gwen, this is your world?"

"I knew you would like it here. You don't have to leave, this can be yours." Gwen's voice, as pleasant as it had been in Sloane's world, was music here. The air was a silken liquid quality that caressed Sloane's skin as she walked.

The trees were of fall hues, but there were no leaves on the ground. The moon was greenish, glowing with as much light as the sun at dusk. The surroundings were un-real but solid to the sight and touch. The stars showered the charcoal sky as pinks, reds, oranges and yellows, with some blazing blue ones. Sloane marveled at this world that was occurring right along with the one she had just left.

"Where are the families, the Fairies?" she asked.

Gwen laughed. "They have to sleep too, they are all in their homes sleeping."

The path they were following was blue, changing from light blue two steps in front of them to dark blue two steps behind.

"Here is my home." Gwen led Sloane to a modest, white-washed cottage with a dark green door and a thatched roof. "You thought a castle?" Gwen laughed.

"I don't know what I thought. This is a strange and beautiful place, but I think I prefer the blue sky, and green grass of my world."

"I know. But now we sleep and in the morning, I will finish the story."

"But—?"

"No buts. I am tired." Gwen pointed to a bed in the corner. "That is where we sleep. I live alone and have only one bed."

Sloane lay beside Gwen, listening to the Faerie

Queen's breathing. *I didn't realize Gwen was so old. She is always so vibrant and full of energy. I didn't know her family was all gone, no wonder she had so much time for me.* She reached over and squeezed Gwen's hand.

"Go to sleep, Sloane, I am all right. We will talk in the morning." And as Gwen squeezed Sloane's hand, Sloane closed her eyes in deep sleep.

The smell of hot porridge and flat bread floating in the air of Gwen's home woke Sloane.

"Good morning, Daughter."

"Good morning, Mother." Both women felt the love of the other, and all was well.

"I will finish telling you of Mouadas, then show you some of my world. You may change your mind, and stay." Gwen handed Sloane a steaming bowl of breakfast porridge.

"Sit and eat with me, Gwen. I wonder how Chullain is doing?"

"He is fine. The time here is what it takes. In your world, it has a span. He will not even know we are gone when you get back. . . . You are going back?" Gwen sat and there was the silence of breakfast being eaten.

"Nuba lived with the shepherds of the valley. It is said his magic caused the sheep to have varying shades of browns, reds, and blacks." Gwen started the story again when they had finished eating.

"Go on. I can listen and clean the bowls at the same time. Here, more tea." Sloane, listening carefully, cleaned up the breakfast from the small table.

"Mouadas had a small but thriving trade selling dyed cloth; she employed orphaned children to weave and dye the cloth."

"That sounds admirable," Sloane said, sitting down.

"Yes, doesn't it? Mouadas did not care for the children. The children lived in squalor and worked long hours. The boys had the miserable job of crushing and soaking the shellfish to extract the dye. The girls ran the looms, and they all dyed the cloth."

There was a long pause. Sloane was getting a little tired from the inactivity, but she felt she had to know why Mouadas had such animosity toward Nuba. "Why did Mouadas hate Nuba?" she asked with her some-times-startling directness.

"Nuba was competition, with his natural-colored wools. And Nuba took children away from Mouadas and gave them a home tending his sheep."

"That is no reason to exile him to the coldness of the mountains." Sloane was feeling something other than understanding for Mouadas now.

"That was not the reason. Nuba fell in love with Mouadas."

"But—I don't understand?" Sloane said.

Gwen took Sloane's hand. "Come walk with me. I will try to explain. There is still more of my world to see while I talk."

The morning sun was white gold in the pastel green sky, fluffy buttermilk blue clouds bunched above the distant rust-colored mountains. Giant birds that Sloane had never seen sailed above, soaring to great heights, then disappearing from view. Gwen's cottage was surrounded by all manner of structure and building. There were tall minaret-type towers; there were long houses, and ornate chalets, there were even grass huts and tents.

Sloane was delighted at her surroundings and forgot for a while the need to find out about Nuba and Mouadas. "I never knew there were so many different types of fairies. When I saw you dancing in the faerie circles, it was all young faeries."

"How better to attract mortals to join the circle. Besides, only the young have the endurance to dance for seven years," Gwen said.

"Where do we walk?" Sloane asked.

"To where you can see Mouadas. We will penetrate the barriers between the faerie world and mortal world." Gwen led Sloane to a large opaque, translucent windmill, whose large fan blades slowly moved in a giant circle of light. Between each section of blades, a scene of some place in the world slipped by. Sloane felt disoriented watching the visible portals to all parts of the world slide by in front of her. Large windows of peoples living in snow houses, peoples living in tents on blowing sands. There were mountains, plains, and exotic cities, green jungles; she was in the center of all time and space, and the entire world was there for her to see.

Gwen stopped the blades with a wave of her hand. Sloane immediately recognized the valley. She saw their hole home and Chullain sleeping in the entrance. The next instant the scene changed, and they were in the valley town. Then they stepped through the thickness of the portal air into a large magnificent room, of tapestries hung, and tall arched windows.

At the end of the room, framed in the light of lead glass window, a mature but very beautiful woman sat. Sloane looked at Gwen. "Can she see us?"

Gwen shook her head no. Sloane boldly closed the distance to the woman, inspecting every aspect of her. Suddenly Mouadas raised her head and looked directly at Sloane.

"Uuuuuhhh," Sloane gasped. Gwen placed her hand on her arm and Sloane realized Mouadas did not see her.

Mouadas was deep in thought; her brow had little worry lines above the white pearl hanging between her eyebrows. She did not like the feeling she was getting. She was feeling agitated, needy; the only thing that masked the feeling was work.

From outside the faint sound of children could be heard. It was not the shouting and laughing of play, it was the talk of tired children working and wondering what they would eat that night. Mouadas quickly went to the window and pulled it shut. She felt their pain, but would not allow her love to surface, to be killed again.

She did not return to the table. She walked between Gwen and Sloane, really through them. She paused and sniffed. *That smell, rain shower and flowers, where have I smelt this before?* She went to a small upright cupboard, pulling a key from her bosom, unlocking the doors. Inside she removed a small cask with gold hinges and silver pulls that had been made into a chest with individual small compartments.

As Sloane and Gwen watched, she removed a lock of shiny black hair tied with gold thread, her eyes filled, and silent tears spilled over and wet her face. Three times she removed locks of black hair, "Meelas," she said for the first and "Boulle," then "Neelas," for the next two. Mouadas's slim body convulsed as grief seized her.

Sloane couldn't help herself; she flew to Mouadas and knelt beside her, embracing her. Mouadas calmed with the unseen presence of Sloane, and she felt a strange warmth that she hadn't felt since she lost her children. She stood, returned the chest, and wiped her eyes with a kerchief pulled from her sleeve.

Sloane knew she was still mourning her children. "She still loves. I am going now, Gwen."

"Yes, you are needed."

Sloane embraced Gwen, stepped through the

silken-aired portal, and back to the entrance to where Chullain lay.

Forty-three—The Old Warrior

Chullain reared up, huffing and slobbering and licking Sloane's face. "I'm glad to see you too. But we spend no more time here. Go find the path to the village."

Without even his whuufff, Chullain was off; he was glad to leave this place. Sloane gathered up her meager belongings, stowing them in her shoulder bag, and strode off after Chullain. She could see Chullain's big furry bottom and bushy tail flagging furiously at one of the last big boulders on the hillside. When she stood beside him, she could see the narrow footpath that meandered down to the twin-rutted road that led past the four cottages she had seen yesterday.

The place seemed subdued; there were few birds flying or singing. Even the leaves of the trees seemed to whisper. The tall grasses swished Sloane's knees as they walked the meandering hill path to the road.

Across the way against the same hillside they were coming down she saw a flock of sheep all gray. The shepherd looked to be a young girl, but the distance was so great it was hard to tell. The fields of barley looked to be a good harvest this year. All the fields were well cared for. The fences made from the rocks found clearing and planting were tight and not falling down.

The first person Sloane was going to meet was just ahead. Þorbjörn, once a fierce raider, now a peaceful farmer, sat on his stone fence putting an edge on his scythe. The sun was warm on his back, and the rasp of the stone against the steel of the scythe brought back many memories of conflicts good and bad. The scythe was not far removed from a weapon, and it felt good, the steel, the stone, the sun, the memories.

When he became aware of Sloane's approach, the stone stopped its rasp and he enjoyed the picture of the beautiful young ginger-haired woman as she walked confidently and gracefully along the twin-rutted road.

Sloane slowed and stopped in front of Þorbjörn. "Good day, sir."

Þorbjörn slid down off the fence and stood as he stood when he was a sea rover. "Good day, mistress. I am Þorbjörn, this is my farm." He swept his skullcap off and stood waiting for Sloane's response.

"Þorbjörn, you have the manner of a warrior of the sea."

Þorbjörn flexed and stood even straighter, "I sailed with Bóðvarr the Brutal. I was third in command of the Blood Fleet of the Ice Sea. But now I raise barley and children." And he again became the yeoman farmer he was, but still stood straight and tall.

"I am Sloane. I have been on a journey from the Deep Forest Grove of Sisters on the other side of the mountain."

"Do you come here? Or do you journey on? Tell me on the way. We'll go to the house and eat and talk. The field will be here tomorrow." Þorbjörn slung his scythe over his shoulder, looked down at Chullain, and said, "You too. Come on, big dog."

Chullain looked at Sloane, and when she moved up beside Þorbjörn, he squeezed in between them, his tail a semaphore of happiness.

"That small field of barley is mine." Þorbjörn pointed to the right, "and that large one of oats, and there on the hillside that is Abaigeal with our flock. Abaigeal is my

105

oldest. Her name means her father's joy. It names her well. She is my joy."

"Will I get to meet her?" Sloane asked; she was very much interested in how much the women of this valley knew of the Goddess.

"Stay the night and you will. She brings the flock to the lower pens and then she comes home for the night. We have four rooms in our home. You will sleep with Abaigeal." Þorbjörn beamed at Sloane as he opened the door to the cottage home that he was so proud of.

Sloane was impressed; this old warrior had a taste for comfortable living. The north wall was all fireplace and hearth, and spinning on a piece of twine was a large shoulder that looked to be beef and smelled of beef. It sizzled and dropped its juices in the black catch pot under it. There was a large pot simmering with an occasional bubble popping on the steaming surface. Sloane couldn't help it; her stomach drove her closer to look and smell.

"Is that bread?" she asked.

"Yes. We will feast on beef and lentils and fresh bread and learn of each other tonight. And beer, we have beer just ready for drinking." Þorbjörn wound the twine so the shoulder would keep spinning, stirred the lentils, and sucked the aromas deep with obvious pride and pleasure.

"What can I do to help? Who is this?" Sloane noticed in the shadowy corner a woman nursing a baby.

"I am Riona, slave to Þorbjörn, and wet nurse to Þorgeirr." The woman started to rise, but Þorbjörn stepped between them and motioned her to remain seated.

"Þorgeirr is my son, his mother died in childbirth. He came late in my life. The others had all made their own lives, except for Abaigeal." Þorbjörn turned, took the baby, and held Þorgeirr close. Sloane could tell he loved the child.

"Riona, are you treated well?" Sloane asked and startled Þorbjörn and Riona with the suddenness and directness of the question. Þorbjörn turned crimson, but to his credit he did not bluster or get angry. He turned to Riona for her reply.

"Yes, mistress, I am well." Riona reached out and took baby Þorgeirr back. "You are of the old religion, aren't you? You are the Seeker?" She dropped a corner of her bodice and Þorgeirr stopped his fussing and nursed noisily. Riona smiled. "He was still hungry."

Þorbjörn stepped close to Sloane; he got even closer and looked piercingly in Sloane's eyes, then he sniffed each shoulder.

He stepped back, "You are welcome here; my mother was of the Mother Goddess." Then he dipped his head, something no man or woman had ever done to her before. Sloane was touched.

Riona, who had been watching, said, "He's a good man."

Þorbjörn stepped back, placing his hand caressingly on Riona's head. The exchange showed they loved. Sloane was satisfied that whatever slavery Riona was in was no worse than most marriages.

"Father, Father, come help." The voice coming from outside did not sound panicked, just anxious.

"That's Abaigeal." Þorbjörn whirled and hurried out the door with Sloane and Chullain right behind.

A pretty brown-haired girl in baggy trews was struggling to carry a yearling lamb that by the red on its wool was hurt. "Father, get the flock in the pens. I'll tend to the lamb."

107

"Chullain, put the sheep in the pen," Sloane said, hurrying to help Abaigeal. Chullain's tail stopped its usual flapping and he looked at Þorbjörn like, how am I supposed to know what to do? But Þorbjörn was already moving among the flock, using Abaigeal's crook, moving the sheep to the pen. Chullain let nature take over, and when he started, they moved the sheep into the pen swiftly.

"Good boy, Chullain, good boy. You earned something special tonight." Þorbjörn roughed the dog up behind his ears and then hurried after the bloody lamb and his daughter.

"What is it, Daughter?"

Sloane had her healing bag opened, and she was closing three gaping slash or cut wounds, two on the left rear flank and one that left the left ear dangling. "What did this, Abaigeal?" Her deft hands moved across the wounds with needle and gut thread, and they closed almost before she cinched the stitch.

"Mistress, are you a healer? The wounds look better already." Abaigeal held the yearling's head in her lap.

"What did this? Abby, tell Sloane what animal did this?" Þorbjörn hung over them. "You weren't threatened, were you? I'll get my bow and if Chullain can go with me. We will hunt and kill this. What are we hunting for, girl?"

"It was a small dragon, Papa. It came out of the rocks near the caves of darkness," Abaigeal said and pointed to the ridge of rock in the dusk-darkening distance.

Sloane finished with the lamb and putting her healing bag in order, stopped and lay her hand on Abaigeal's hand. "Are you sure it was a dragon?"

"What did the dragon look like? Did it breathe fire?" Þorbjörn bent down to reexamine the wounds. "Mistress Sloane, what caused the wounds?"

"The two on the flank are claw, and head and ear is from fang," Sloane said.

"How do you know this?"

"Abaigeal, how did the dragon attack the lamb?"

"It dashed from a rock pile, grabbed the lamb's rear, and pulled itself on top, biting as it went.—It had a long tail—and big hooked claws, and maybe baby wings " Abaigeal told what she saw without hysterics. This impressed Sloane.

"Why did the dragon let go?" Abaigeal's father asked.

"I hit it on the baby wings, and it squealed, flapped them like it was trying to fly, and it fell off and scrambled in to the rocks." Again Abaigeal told her story solemnly and matter-of-factly.

"You are a brave girl, Abaigeal. Þorbjörn, you can be proud of your daughter; she fought as a warrior." Sloane set the lamb up so Abaigeal could stand and accept the embrace of her father. The yearling lamb tottered off, baa-baa, toward the sheep in the pen.

Riona stood in the door. "Come, the baby is fed and asleep, and the food is on the table."

Forty-four—Þorbjörn's Surprise Marriage

They sat at the large table in the manner of the Norse. Þorbjörn sat at the head; his was a large silver bowl to eat from. Sloane as guest sat next to him, her rather shallow bowl was of wood as was Abaigeal's, and Riona's. Each bowl had one rather shovellike wooden spoon; the other eating utensil was the belt knife everyone carried.

Sloane stood behind the stool. Þorbjörn pointed out for her to sit. "Who normally sits here?" she asked.

"Helgi sat there until she died," Þorbjörn said.

"Has any person taken over all her duties? All of them?" Sloane looked directly at the old warrior.

Abaigeal could see where this was going and since Helgi had not been her mother, she grinned at her now squirming father.

"Riona," he said and he could not return Sloane's gaze.

"Then you know what you must do." Sloane said. "Warrior Honor demands it." She stepped away from the stool in front of her.

Poor old Þorbjörn was torn between what he knew was right and the customs of the land. He conquered his embarrassment, and he stood tall and walked around the table to Riona. "Come, wife," he said, holding out his arm, and he escorted her to her place at the table.

Riona reached up and kissed the grizzled old warrior, "Yes, husband," was all she said.

Sloane took Riona's place, and Þorbjörn beaming now said, "Eat, eat, this is our wedding feast." He cut great hunks of meat off the whole shoulder lying in the middle of the table and carried them to each woman at the table, Riona first, of course.

*   *   *

After the meal Riona and Þorbjörn retired to the bedroom with the door. And as Abaigeal and Sloane went outside under the stars, the moon was the barest sliver of light like a coin almost buried in the sand.

"Let's not go too far. I want to be able to hear Þorgeirr," Abaigeal said.

"Riona will hear him before you. Come, let's sit on the

fence." Sloane tugged her sleeve. "I want to hear of this dragon."

"It just ran out of the rocks, attacked the lamb, and went back."

"Have you lost any lambs before?" Sloane breathed the air with the faint taint of sheep, "Listen, you can hear the oats whispering." A small ground breeze from the east was making the oats in the field brush against each other.

"Mistress—Sloane, are you a sorcerer? I have lived here for ten years and I have never heard the oats whisper." Abaigeal looked with growing awe at this beautiful young woman only years older than she was.

*　　*　　*

Sloane's laughter wafted out on the slight easterly air currents blending with the rustling from the oat fields. The Goddess sent this breeze. Sloane's laughter traveled through time and space and fell on the ears of Cillian, sitting in the masthead of yet another raiding long boat. This time his. The *Rowyn* (Red Headed in Old Irish), his ship, had no wind and was lying becalmed. Cillian was in the masthead looking for water disturbance, clouds, anything to denote wind. When the first kiss of the easterly caressed his cheek, the laughter he had heard once again brought a tumult to his soul. He sat and let the fluttery feeling subside, then he bellowed to the deck. "Snorri, Brundr, more sail, we have the wind." Somehow he knew.

Forty-five—The Dragon

Sloane's laughter tinkled out, and she took Abaigeal's hand. "I am a follower of the Goddess, some call me a Priestess. I am but a young woman not much older than you."

"But you know so much. You are not afraid," Abaigeal said.

"I was taught by the women of the island, and the Goddess protects me. Come here." Sloane slid down from her perch on the stone fence. She took Abaigeal's face in both hands and looked into her brown eyes, into her soul. Sloane kissed her and said, "Come tell me more of this dragon we are going to slay.—This is the first of many adventures of your life.—Now what color were the scales? It did have scales? The feet, what color were they?"

Abaigeal clapped her hands. "We are going to slay the dragon?—The scales looked soft, and the feet. The feet. It only had two. Only two feet."

Sloane saw Abaigeal's eyes widen with the memory of the beast that attacked the lamb.

"Sloane, it ran like a chicken."

"I must see this dragon. I think I know what it is.—Let's get some sleep, and I'll go with you in the morning." They walked back to the farmhouse through the quiet of the night.

"You know what it is? Have you seen it before?" Abaigeal asked.

"Not this one, but I think I have seen a bigger version. I saw it slain by a Norse Raider." Sloane said. Her voice had changed just slightly when she said Norse Raider, but Abaigeal caught it.

"You care for this raider?—What is his name?"

112

Sloane smiled, the picture of Cillian etched in her psyche. "No. He is just a Raider. He is called Cillian."

"I think there is more, and you must tell me tomorrow when we slay the Dragon." Abaigeal said as they crawled into the same sleeping pallet.

"Good night," Riona said from the chair where she was nursing Þorgeirr.

"Good night Riona." And the sound of the baby suckling was the last thing Sloane heard that night.

Morning came early, as it always has on a farm. Sloane did not know what time Riona got up and started duties. "Being the good wife isn't any different than being the good slave is it, Riona?"

Riona, straightened up from the hearth, had a rueful look, "No, mistress, being a house wife is slavery after a fashion. But I choose it. What else is there?"

Þorbjörn listened but kept silent as he sorted through his war arrows, picking the very best for the dragon he intended on slaying today. When he sensed he should say something, he looked across the room at them and said, "These five arrows will do the job." And he grinned at them.

Riona's shoulders moved as if to shrug and said, "He is a good man." Sloane was the only one who heard her. She put her hand on Riona's shoulder and moved to the table where Þorbjörn was working.

"Þorbjörn. Abaigeal and I will go after the dragon. You have that field of oats that must be cut."

"You are girls. I am a warrior—"

And Sloane cut him off with, "You are also a farmer and what will happen to oats if you don't harvest them?"

"The birds, the winds, the oats fall to the ground and most rot.—You are right take my war bow.—And use that great dog of yours, he can help." Þorbjörn without a look back stopped outside the door, shouldered his scythe, and walked to the field.

"I didn't think he would let us," Abaigeal said.

"He senses change. He told me so last night. He is a good man, but he thinks only one way; this is hard for him," Riona said setting two bowls of gruel on the table for them.

As they ate, Sloane asked, "Where will I find Mouadas after we take care of this dragon?"

The pause and silence after her question caused Sloane to look at Riona and Abaigeal questioningly.

Finally Riona asked, "Why do you want to see Mouadas?"

"Yes. Why? Do you know her?" Abaigeal's enthusiasm was dampened by Mouadas's name.

"No, but I must meet her after we rid your valley of the dragon." Sloane stood. "Chullain, up, we need your nose."

"Do we take Father's bow?"

"Can you draw it?"

"No."

"Then neither can I. We won't need it."

As they walked the steadily steeper path to the hillside pastures, Abaigeal pointed out a neighboring pasture. "That was Nuba's until Mouadas took it. She tried to take ours, but when Mother died, she left us alone."

"Did you know this Nuba well?" Sloane asked.

"Oh, yes, he was black, you know. I never did understand how that happened. He said his mother and father were black too. Can you imagine that?" Abaigeal stopped. "There, see that jumble of flat rocks. The dragon came from there, and went back there.—Do you think he is still there?"

Sloane sniffed the smell from the beach; the stench of death lay heavy in the morning air. "You say you haven't lost any lambs?" she said, cautiously edging toward the death-smelling rock pile.

"No.—Do you think we should get this close?" Abaigeal asked.

"From the smell I don't think we are in any danger. Did you smell this yesterday?" Sloane stopped cubits from the opening, "Give me your shepherd's crook."

Abaigeal handed her the crook. "Maybe, but it wasn't as bad. There was a wind yesterday. There is none today."

"Awwggkk" came weakly from the opening in the rocks.

"What's that?"

"That's your dragon." Sloane said and pushed the rock with the crook and it tilted off balance and fell.

"Awwggkk, Awwg." The dragon was not fearsome. It did not even look like a dragon now. It could not even hold up the heavy, ugly head on the end of the skinny snake-like neck.

"A Slazoo baby," Sloane said. "It's starving to death. Look, there were two. The other one is in the back. This one killed and ate it."

"He is hurt real bad too. Look at the wound on his belly," Abaigeal said.

"He has been feeding on his own body," Sloane said. "As mean and hateful as they are, this is sad."

Chullain interjected himself between the baby Slazoo and the girls. Both girls heard, "Turn around and back down the hill. I will take care of this. Go!"

Sloane took Abaigeal's hand, and they both walked back the way they came. They did not look back at the muffled thumps and feeble "Awwwgh."

Chullain walked past them. Sloan saw several small

black feathers around his muzzle, "Come here, Chullain." She kept walking to where Chullain had stopped. He still faced down the hill. She knelt beside him, pulled the feathers out of his hair, and wiped the reddish smears off of his muzzle. They did not speak, but they felt each other's pain at what had to be done. Sloane hugged him close and let him know it was all right.

"Did he—?" Abaigeal started to ask but stopped. She knew.

"Yes. The Slazoo would not have survived without its mother. This had to be done," Sloane said, still kneading Chullain's ears and head.

"It's done on the farm at times. I never liked it, but I have helped sheep and lambs who were too sick." Abaigeal said.

"It is not cruel. The Mother understands relieving the pain of her creatures."

"Mistress, mistress," came floating up the hill to them. Þorbjörn started trotting up the hill to them, remarkably agile for the years he carried.

He stopped in front of them slightly winded; he held his war bow, "I've come to help."

Abaigeal smiled. "Papa, Chullain killed the Slazoo. It's all over."

"Þorbjörn, have you seen or heard of gigantic vulture-headed eagles here before?" Sloane asked. "Because it was no dragon. It was a fledgling Slazoo. That is what I heard it called."

"I have seen great shadows on the sun before, and cattle, sometimes a man would disappear. The legend I heard was the Slazoo, that is what they called it too, would raise its young here every twenty years, then leave." Þorbjörn recounted. "It always returned, though."

Forty-six—Sloane Visits Mouadas

Sloane said her good-byes to Riona and þorbjörn at the gate to the farmhouse. Abaigeal walked partway with her to the town called Twill.

There were two hills before the road entered Twill. Abaigeal and Sloane stood on the second one, and Twill lay before them. "That tall building in the center that is the church. That taller building at the far edge of town, that is where you will find Mouadas." Abaigeal pointed the structures out.

Sloane smiled at the thought that Mouadas would have a home taller than the church. "Is there a Shrine to the Goddess in this valley?" she asked.

"I heard there used to be a shrine at the spring."

"Where is the spring?"

"Mouadas uses it for the dying process for her cloth. Her house sets on it.—I wish I were coming with you," Abaigeal said.

"You are needed on the farm. I talked to your father, and he is going to look for help. When he finds someone, you can come to me." Sloane embraced the young woman. "Come as soon as you can," she said.

Abigail watched as Sloane and Chullain again headed into an unknown.

The road began to get busier, almost all traffic, carts and foot were going into Twill. Sloane's striking beauty and the great beast of a dog Chullain caused a ripple that passed though the crowd and got to Twill before them. They were almost a parade when they did, and town folk and shopkeepers stared at them.

Sloane acknowledged those who greeted her with smiles, raising her hand in the timeless salute of friendship.

117

The town dogs did not come out barking and begging as usual, they slunk along the sides of the road watching. When one started to cross in front of them, a low growl from Chullain sent him scurrying back.

"Be friendly, Chullain, this will be our home for a while," Sloane said. Then her attention was drawn from the dogs to a slender woman in flowing purple robes directing children who appeared to be standing and wading in wine.

Both women became aware of each other at the same instant. Mouadas stood on the edge of the purple pool. She had to shade her eyes from the sun to see Sloane who was coming in with the sun.

Mouadas felt the first pangs of change, the unease that something was going to change her life.

The regal beauty of the Dark Woman struck Sloane. "I am Sloane, follower of the Goddess. This is Chullain, companion and friend."

"Why have you come? Do you want to purchase?" Mouadas did not want this conversation. She did not want change.

"You are Mouadas. I have come to see you," Sloane said and she walked off the road, and around the purple pool to where Mouadas stood.

The children had stopped treading the cloth in the dye pit and were watching the drama unfolding. "Get back to work!" But Mouadas's words did not have the ring of authority that they used to. The children went from one foot to the other, treading the cloth in to the purple dye. Their legs were stained purple, some of the smaller ones up to the waist.

"I did not invite you here." Mouadas stood her ground. She neither advanced to greet nor retreated from Sloane.

"I was sent. You did not invite me; but you will grant me the hospitality of your land as a traveler guest." Sloane was standing directly in front of Mouadas now. She had to look up to look in the almond-gray eyes.

"You know me, and you know the customs of my land. What else do you know of me?—Work!" She broke of her conversation with Sloane to yell at the watching children. "Come with me. I once was a priestess. . . ."

"Mouadas."

"Yes.—Aren't you coming?"

"Mistress Mouadas, please. The children should come out of the dye pool for a while." Sloane entreated the willowy, exotic, dark woman.

Mouadas felt the pull of Sloane's goodness. "Oh, very well. Out! Out! Bring the cloth out. Hang it on the drying racks. The rest of the day is holiday."

The children stopped, now gaping, astonishment giving way to joy as they snuck glances at each other, picking the hanks of wet dripping cloth. They were afraid that Mouadas would change her mind.

"You have hard-working children," Sloane said, knowing she was going to get a response but not knowing what kind.

Mouadas was watching the children scamper off, giggling trying to be quiet. "My children are dead or slaves."

Her words chilled Sloane, who now wished she had not said anything. "I am sorry, Mouadas. I never knew my birth mother. But many women have raised and nurtured me these years."

"I am not cruel to the children."

"I can see that. But they may need more in love and instruction than they are getting now?"

"They are orphans. If not for me, they would be slaves, or working as servants on a farm." Mouadas stopped, turned to Sloane, and again said. "I am not cruel."

"No. You are not. Come show me where I stay this night." Sloane took Mouadas's hand. She felt a power that said Mouadas would accept her.

Mouadas brought the hand that took hers to eye level and examined it. "You have the callused hand of someone who knows the ways of a loom. Yes. You should stay. I feel you bear me a message I must listen to."

They entered the tall slender tower of a structure that Mouadas had built and called home. The entrance door itself was low and narrow. Mouadas bent and entered first, then Sloane followed, twisting slightly to fit through.

"Only one attacker at a time, eh?" Mouadas said. "And he would soon block it with his body."

Sloane stood up in a circular room adorned by tapestries hanging on the walls. A tight spiral staircase shafted the center of the room to the minaret-like top of the structure. The floor was blue and slick and shiny as a glacier. When Sloane had turned completely around and started breathing normally, Mouadas pulled her to the portion of the wall that had no tapestry.

"This is what you seek."

Sloane stepped past the large rough-hewn pillar that erupted from the floor. "Ooohh, I never expected this."

The rough-hewn pillar was a living Oak. The area between the pillar and the wall appeared small until you stepped past it. On the Oak side was a Sacred Grove. The spring bubbled and sprayed upwards from the center of a rock-lined pool.

Sloane waded out to the center of the pool and let the water cascade over her. "Come in, Mouadas," she entreated, holding out her hands.

"No. Not for a long time. Maybe some time, but not now," Mouadas said. She enjoyed seeing Sloane in the water. She hadn't enjoyed anything for a long time. Not since—. "No, not this time. Soon I think.—Soon.—Though."

As Sloane splashed her way back to Mouadas, she noticed the spring water was the floor of Mouadas's home. "I have seen a floor like this not long ago, only it was air and not water under it," she said, taking Mouadas's hand and stepping out.

"There is only one who does such things," Mouadas said, handing Sloane drying towels, "And he left."

Mouadas gave Sloane a look that challenged her to dispute what she had just said. Sloane seemed not to notice and continued drying herself.

"Those are magic waters, you know. If I lived here, I would bathe in them every day." Sloane said.

"I bathe every day." Mouadas's icy return still did not cause Sloane any concern.

"I know you do. Come, show me the rest and tell me about this magic floor over the spring waters." Sloane slipped her arm through Mouadas's and guided her back around the tree pillar to the spiral staircase.

"You do like me, you know. I am what you were and can be again," Sloane said gently.

"Yes. But I do not want to change. I have my walls that I have built. I am happy behind them. There are no surprises.—You are going to change all this aren't you?"

"Of course, things are going to change, nothing stays the same. Does it?—This is beautiful: you have already rebuilt this shrine." Sloane skipped across the floor and peeked out the slit of window.

Mouadas couldn't help herself: she felt lightened and maybe even happy as she joined Sloane. "See over there, the children are playing in the meadow." She fell silent, wondering why she hadn't watched them play before.

"Who cooks for them?" Sloane asked.

"My cooks prepare one meal a day for them."

"One meal? When is it served? Let's eat with them?" Sloane said. "It will be fun like a party."

"No. I can't," Mouadas said; she held up her hands "No.—Come, I will show you where you will stay."

Sloane followed Mouadas up the spiral stairs to the next partial floor. It only went partway around the complete circle of the structure. It was open above the Sacred Grove and the Oak that grew there.

"Mouadas. Is this Sacred Water and this Sacred Oak, are they why you built and stayed here?" Sloane's compassion welled over into her words.—"Why did Nuba leave?"

"Not now, Sloane.—I must be alone.—Go eat with the children. I will join you later," Mouadas said. She embraced Sloane. "You are going to turn my life upside down again, aren't you? Take your great dog and join the children. I will have the cook serve something special. Go!"

Sloane didn't question the words or the tone; she knew the Goddess was talking to Mouadas.

Forty-seven—The Children

The children were housed in a low and longish structure of rocks and logs with thatched roof. It was like all of the out buildings in the area.

Sloane was just in time as the cook ladled out bowls of gruel for children. "Is there no milk to drink?" she asked the cook, a grandmotherly woman old before her time. The cook shook her head no.

"What are you called?" Sloane asked her.

"Grunda, mistress," she answered, not looking at Sloane.

"Can you get milk?"

"Yes, ma'am, at the farmers market."

"Get some," Sloane said, "I'll finish here." And she took the ladle and began filling bowls. "Get some honey too!" she shouted to the cook. "And some sausages!"

A little blue-stained boy, with dirty hair, face, and hands held out his bowl. His eyes were big in wonder at this beautiful fire-haired woman standing in front of him.

"What's your name? How'd you get so dirty?—All girls older that eight, come here," Sloane said to the children. Three girls slowly stood up and came forward.

"I am Eily. I am ten. That is Gemma, she is eight, and Doreen is also eight."

"Let me see your hands.—Turn them over, now your elbows." The girls did as Sloane asked. Then they put their hands behind them and stood waiting.

"Eily, you girls take the children to wherever you clean up, and wash them. Scrub them clean. Then come back and we will eat."

"But I'm hungry now," the little boy whined.

"I know but you don't eat until you are clean. Now go."

Sloane walked through the dim rather dingy quarters the children lived in. The beds were disreputable, and smelly. All needed new bedding.

Oh, Mouadas, how could you not take more interest in these children? She began ripping up the bedding and dragging the pallets outside to air.

"Mistress, I have milk, honey, and sausages."

Grunda returned laden with pitcher and baskets, and the start of a smile on her broad pleasant face.

"Good, set the table. Prepare yourself a place. The children will be back and we will feast.—Set a place for Mouadas too," Sloane said. Whirling she ran out the door, jumping over the pile of dirty bedding, running to get Mouadas.

Grunda's face lost part of its smile. "Mouadas is coming. I'll believe that when I see her."

As Sloane ran up the path to the tower house, Mouadas completed her prayers, her first in many years. As she stood up, the Goddess embraced her and slid into the ethers of time, vanishing from sight, her presence still felt.

"Mouadas, come, you must come," Sloane shouted as she bent to enter the house.

She straightened up as Mouadas slipped through first and stood in front of her.

"Mouadas. Mouadas—Wha—Mouadas, you've been with the Goddess. I can see it . . . and I can smell the Flowers of Goodness." Sloane reached out, and then pulled back; sometimes it was not good to disrupt the Aura of another.

"It is good, for the first time in years, it is good. Embrace me, Sloane. I need the feel and love of people now." And the dark woman reached out to Sloane.

Grunda's look of concern vanished into a wide-open smile as she examined Mouadas's face as they approached, and saw none of the bitterness that used to cloud her features. She dropped a small curtsey and said, "Your place is ready, mistress."

The chatter and laughter coming from the clean-scrubbed children stopped when Mouadas entered.

They lowered their heads and sat in bowed uncomfortable silence.

The dirty little boy now sparkling white but still speckled with blue spots pulled on Eily's arm and whispered to her.

"Selig, what do you want?" Mouadas asked. "Do you want to eat now?"

Selig's head bobbed enthusiastically.

"Go ahead and eat, Selig. All of you eat."

All the children looked to Eily, who looked questioning to Mouadas, who smiled and nodded yes.

Eily said, "Eat, Selig. Everybody eat," and she speared a sausage and stuffed it her mouth, grease bubbling out and running down her chin.

Sloane ate sparingly. When finished she brought her harp to the table, and the woodland melodies brought the softened heart of Mouadas to the full state of Goddess love.

Mouadas and Grunda stayed with the children that evening, making the quarters more livable.

Sloane went back to the tower home and walked the spiral stairs to the very top. She looked back for Chullain, who was lying at the first step watching her.

"Aren't you coming?"

Chullain whuffed his no and laid his head down for a nap.

Sloane stepped on the stairs; they rose each time her feet were set. Soon she was spiraling up through rooms that were splendid with the culture of the peoples of the burning sand and giant stone pyramids. Some reflected the islands of the great blue Mediterranean.

I must examine these one day. The light was muted dim but luminescent at the very top of Mouadas's tower. She looked out over the darkened countryside; a faint sliver of the road was visible and right below her she could see Mouadas and Grunda returning from putting the children to bed.

Mouadas stopped and raised her eyes to where Sloane leaned out of the larger shuttered opening. "Look to the mountains," she said.

"You said something, mistress?" Grunda asked.

"No. Nothing, Grunda. We move the children in the tower tomorrow."

"Mistress, why are you doing this after so many years of not caring?"

The women were at the low narrow door, and Mouadas stopped and answered before she entered. "It is time. I was dead with my children. Now I must live with my new children. The Goddess never left me. She has my children now and given me care of these."

Grunda did not know what Mouadas was talking about, but she was happy with the change in her mistress.

Forty-eight—Shape Shifting

Sloane was gazing at the mountains, just as Mouadas had said. They rose in the distance visible only by the lightness of the snow on the peaks, breaking the stark blackness of the night as a lighter shade.

Why does she want me to look to the mountains? Then she saw it, a glow on the east slope near the peak. It pulsated a lonely light in the black of the mountainous night.

"Hooo hoooo," came from the opposite window. Sloane left the pull of the pulsating glow and saw a large gray-white owl sitting on the ledge. "Hooo," and the great round golden globes for eyes opened and closed.

Sloane walked closer to the bird. "Who are you, Owl? Do you know me? Who sent you?"

The Owl just sat there, shook his wings out once, and settled those all-seeing eyes on Sloane.

Sloane touched his soft neck feathers and thought, *I would like to fly and see like you.*

She felt the rippling of her skin her eyes began to see farther; everything was more distinct. She was on the floor looking up. The owl in the window said, "Come up, Sloane. It is easy, just a couple beats of your wings."

Sloane looked down past her belly of feathers and saw her yellow-taloned feet; she looked along her arms and saw powerful-feathered wings.

Three beats of her wings, and she settled rather clumsily by the owl in the window. "Nuba, is that you?"

"Of course. I will soon be returning here as Nuba. Mouadas will need me soon. Come, I will show you something." And Nuba the big owl turned and stepped out the window, falling ten feet before his big wings bit into the air and with a fluffing-fluffing sound, raised him again. "Come. Sloane, step out. You know you can do it!"

And Sloane stepped out, working her wings, and they caught the air and, fluff-fluff, raised her up alongside of Nuba. "This is good. Go, I will follow."

They flew low, skimming the ground. Sloane circled Riona and Þorbjörn's farm, and sailed low in front of Abaigeal, who was standing in the yard gazing skyward. "Sloane, that is you. I know it is Sloane. Fly, Sloane, into the stars into the magic of the night. I will follow." Sloane swooped low one last time, then followed Nuba high into the stars.

Nuba settled into a low glide, indicating a seacoast

town. "That is Norns. Your destiny is going to take a turn here." Then Nuba angled into a steep climb, and Sloane followed.

"Where?" she whispered over the cold of the night and sound of their feathers as they ruffled the sky.

"There." And Nuba folded his wings and dove in to the darkness.

Sloane just saw the shapes of five longboats pulled up on the beach and the fires of the camp when she folded her wings and followed Nuba into plummeting dive. She cupped her wings and pushed the air rapidly to land softly beside him on the rocks above a softly flickering fire about to die out.

"Raiders," she said.

"A special raider." Nuba grunted. "Look."

There off from the others with a small fire for warmth and a torch for light Cillian sat. He was running a stone on the blade of his throwing ax.

"He is thinking of you," Nuba said.

"How do you know this? And how do you know of him and me?" Sloane asked, edging closer to the small fire.

"I am Nuba, trained by my Mother. The Mother of all to know these things."

"Whhooo," Sloane said.

Cillian peered into the darkness.

"You can not speak to him in shape-shifted form," Nuba said.

Sloane the owl lifted off the great stone and settled on Cillian's pile of equipment, his short buckler. The muffled feather sound of her wings alerted Cillian to her presence. There in the dim shadowy light of the driftwood fire, a great Snow Owl sat on his breastplate. Her big golden eyes took him in; he felt as if he was being read like one of the big Bibles he had seen in the monasteries they raided.

"Whhhooo."

"Yes, who are you? I know you are not an Owl," Cillian said.

Sloane hopped down and walked closer to the man who possessed her dreams. Owls do not walk gracefully. Cillian extended his ax, and Sloane stepped on it. Cillian brought the ax to his knee, and rested it there.

They examined each other. *He is amazingly gentle for so fierce a warrior,* Sloane thought.

"Are you a messenger from her? Yes, you are of the ginger-hair, aren't you?" Cillian did not touch the owl, he just looked in the giant round orbs of intelligence and mystery. He felt himself drowning in them.

"Take a message to her for me. Tell her I must see her. I must know her. Tell her she haunts me," Cillian entreated the Owl.

Sloane extended her wings for flight, and the tips of her flight feathers brushed his cheek and with a whuf-whuuf of her wings, she was gone.

Cillian felt the touch of Sloane's fingers and held his cheek with one hand, his heart in a softened, confused state he was not used to.

The only sound was the wind and ripples in the air of their wings. Silence that chewed and gnawed at Sloane, she did not like the feelings of attraction that she felt for Cillian.

They both cupped wings and settled into the open window in Mouadas's tower.

"There you are. I have been waiting." Mouadas sat at a small loom, weaving as she waited. "No, don't go. Nuba, stay I have something to say."

Nuba spread his wings and floated from window to floor, and Sloane followed him down. He seemed to stretch, then the feather flowed into dark black skin, and he shot to his full height of a head taller than Mouadas.

"You are looking well, Nuba," Mouadas said.

Nuba, renowned sorcerer, had no words for the woman he was enamored of. He just grinned his dopey jug-eared smile at her, and blushed.

Sloane's shape shifted to her beautiful self, but kept her silence and watched the interplay between the man and woman in the room with her.

Nuba kept his distance as Mouadas stepped closer to him; soon he was against the window ledge again.

"You will have to take the form of the Owl if you try to go further." Mouadas said. "We never talked before. We were always in competition. I think that should change."

"I never wanted competition. I wanted you," Nuba said, his voice strong with conviction of his love.

"I know. I was afraid. I am still afraid, but I want more than the fear," Mouadas said. "Can this be a new beginning?"

"Yes. New beginnings. I am going to my mountain and will be back when the moon is again full for the new beginning." And he was gone.

"He will be back. He is in love with you," Sloane said.

"What is love? When he returns, we will share life and the responsibilities for the children, and this shrine. I may learn what love is again, but for now we will share." Mouadas took Sloane by the arm and led her down the stairs.

When they were both on the stairs, the stairs descended stopping on the second floor of the tower.

"Your room there has basin and water to clean up in. May the Goddess give you dreams and directions this night." Mouadas embraced Sloane, went to the door to her room, entering without looking back.

Forty-nine—-The Shrine of Twill

The next morning and all the following mornings found Mouadas busy. She changed her mind about the children living in the tower. She decided she would live in the long house with them; workers were hired to make it a home for them.

Abaigeal showed up one morning and was welcomed by Mouadas and Sloane. Sloane felt her job was complete there. Mouadas was energized with the children, her business, and the tower, which was an exclusive shrine to the Goddess now.

The moon filled to its fullest, and Nuba arrived, with a flock of many-hued sheep. With the first initial shy welcoming, things began to take on a normalcy, Nuba and some of the children cared for the sheep, in the hillside pastures, and Mouadas appointed Grunda to oversee the dying of the cloth.

Sloane instructed Abaigeal in the ways of the Goddess, until one morning Mouadas said to her, "Sloane, it is time. I will continue what you have started and Abaigeal will be the keeper of the Shrine."

"Yes, you are right. I must journey to Norns," Sloane answered.

"Not just yet, there are things I must pass on to you. Come with me to the Sacred Pool.—You too, Abby. I have much to tell you, go get Eily, Doreen and Gemma. Bring them to the Pool."

Once at the Pool, Mouadas led them in the simple prayers of her country. Then Sloane added those taught her by her mothers on the island, and her mothers of the other shrines. The young girls were becoming initiates in the goodness of the Goddess.

Mouadas beckoned to Sloane, and they left the girls with Abaigeal teaching them of cleanliness and hygiene.

"This is good. You know I did not want you to come here," Mouadas said.

"Yes, I know. But Nuba sent me. And Nuba is close to the Mother."

"He always tried to help. I wouldn't let him," Mouadas admitted.

"That's all changed now. He is staying in the long house some nights I see," Sloane said.

Mouadas smiled and said nothing.

"I am going to Norns from here. Can you tell me anything about it?" Sloane asked.

"It is a port, seven to eight days walk from here depending on the weather. You will have to pass through several little hamlets, and you will be walking into Black Haarald's lands. The Norsemen like to rest up in the little village just south of Norns. It had no name; it is usually called the Norse Rest." Mouadas paused. "It would be best if you disguised your beauty when close to the Norse camp, and hide the fact that you are a priestess. Black Haarald leads the Skirniri."

"I know the Skirniri," Sloane said.

Mouadas looked at her and said, "From your tone I think you must. They are evil, stay away from them.—Come, I have gifts for you."

They went up two sections of stairs. "This is where I weave special cloth. Like this shawl." And she handed Sloane the shawl; it was heavy green with black and brown squares running through it.

Sloane took it with disappointment evident.

"You thought it should be purple or blue or some other rare color?" Mouadas asked. She couldn't help herself; she was almost laughing at Sloane's disappointment.

"Come over to the bronze." She led Sloane to a large polished bronze mirror. "Now put the shawl on and tell me how it looks."

Mouadas helped pull the shawl over Sloane's shoulders and up over her head.

"Ooohh!" Sloane watched as she disappeared as the shawl covered her.

"Yes. That is the shawl of invisibility. Use it wisely and it will not fail you," Mouadas said. "It is warm too."

"Can I wear it and not be invisible?"

"Yes, from now on, it answers only you. The first command was mine."

"I am not going to say good-bye. I am leaving at the dark. Chullain and I will sleep along the road tonight. It will be good to be on a journey with him."

But there was a dinner, and Sloane and Chullain were sent on their way well fed and full of warm thoughts.

He paused in his scouting every so often, walking beside his beloved Sloane, licking her hand when she rested it on his head.

"Find us a place to rest, Chullain, something hidden," Sloane said. The black of the night was diluting to gray. The green, orange, and sometimes red watching eyes of the night hunters along the road edge were no longer there. It would be first light soon, and Sloane wanted to get some rest.

They were in a well-forested area of the road now; the trees grew to the road's edge. Chullain's tail could be seen swinging slowly. Foliage and shrubs hid the rest of his body. "What do you see?" Sloane asked, as she stepped off the road to look.

"Perfect." It was an abandoned holding pen for stock making an overnight trip to Norns or Twill. All evidence of animals was gone, so it was pretty clean, and there was a spring for water close by. There was even a lean-to shelter almost fallen in, but easily repaired.

In less than an hour, Sloane had repaired the lean-to and refreshed herself. "Come on in, boy, you can rest here too."

They slept until the sun was making short tree shadows on the road. The road traffic was very light this day and had not disturbed them. Before they set out, Sloane retrieved some of the soft cheese that Twill was becoming famous for, and some dark bread. They ate all, but left enough for a small meal in an emergency. Sloane wrapped it up in a skin and put it back in her bag.

Fifty—Sloane's Hair

The sun was one huge red half-ball, sliding between the peaks of the mountains over Sloane's left shoulder. Chullain was like a puppy; he was running up and back and circling her as she walked.

Whuufff! Whuufff. His great pink tongue was dangling, and he jumped up on Sloane and kissed her all over her face.

Sloane laughed and hugged him. "I missed you too, boy. It is time we went adventuring again."

A great gray owl flew over them and circled them, the fluff-fluffing of his wings comforting somehow to Sloane. "Good-bye, Nuba, I shall never forget you." And the wings fluffed away, and they walked in the quickening darkness in silence, and some sadness crept into Sloane's thoughts. *I am always leaving, it seems.*

But it felt good, too. No more of almost the same

thing every day. This was freedom. Sloane didn't know if she would ever give up or wanted to give up.

Her leg muscles tightened, then loosened up with the long stride she managed with really very average but attractive legs. Soon her body hit its rhythm, and the miles fell behind them. Chullain too was glad to be out and away from others and to have Sloane all to himself. He ranged up and back and to the sides, always watching, alert for any dangers.

When she was refilling her water bottle, she saw her long ginger-red hair in her reflection. She remembered Mouadas's warning about disguising herself. *What am I going to do about this hair?*

Chullain sat near, his head cocked to one side watching. He got up and walked to her side nuzzling her side, and pulled out her short knife. He sat there with it in his mouth, offering it to her.

"Yes. Yes, you are right, it will grow back, won't it?" Sloane, without looking at her reflection again, drew the sharp blade across large handfuls of her hair until it hung raggedly to just below her ears. Then she gathered up bean pods left from feed for the animals kept there once. She pounded them into powder and made paste that she rubbed in her hair and her face and arms.

"It will be dark when we get on the road again, Chullain," she said as she rinsed the mess off her skin and out of her hair.

"Well, how do I look?" she asked Chullain.

He whimpered and nuzzled her, showing her he still loved her even if she looked like a dark boy with brownish scraggly hair.

"That bad, huh? Too bad it is dark. I would like to see what I look like now." Sloane shouldered her bag, stepped through the underbrush, and out on the road.

Fifty-one—Nuba's Gift

She fell in behind a tinker's wagon and walked the first couple of miles to the jingle and clang of steel and copper pots. The wagon pulled off the road into hostel and they walked on alone.

She noticed two glowing eyes ahead and the closer she got to them, she could see they were high and not moving, except for occasionally going out the coming back.

Whhoooo.

"Hello, Nuba, still protecting us?" Sloane stopped under the barely visible great owl sitting on a branch overhanging the road.

With only whhuuuff whhuuuffing of cupped wings, Nuba settled to the road in front of Sloane. He took one owl step to her, his big eyes closed in a wink, and the feathers stretched into skin and clothes, and Nuba stood there.

His big-eared, long face was happy at seeing Sloane. "You are still beautiful in a rather boyish manner, and you are almost as dark as me. But I would know your spirit anywhere."

Sloane stepped into his fatherly embrace, truly glad to see him. "Why are you watching us? Are we in danger?"

"No, I wanted to give you something I should have given you long ago." Nuba handed her a small pouch. "Inside are two compartments; one has three gold coins you can cut up and use for money when you need to. The other is the black tar of the poppy; use this to deaden pain in those truly hurt. You can also use it when there is no hope for healing and it will be best to sleep."

"Thank you, Nuba. How is it with you and Mouadas and the children?" Sloane asked.

But Nuba was already in owl form and in a lumbering run, his big wings biting the air, he lifted off and Sloane saw him once as he passed on the front of a half moon.

Sloane tied Nuba's pouch's pull string together and slipped it over her head where it hung safely between her breasts.

Then they started walking the dark silent road between the darting eyes of the night animals and sometimes the scurrying, scratching sound of clawed feet along the road edge and in front of them. Chullain followed them with eyes and ears but did not challenge any of the noises.

They walked until the sun was pinking the eastern sky and a sea bird's shriek told Sloane they were near the coast.

"Let us find shelter again, Chullain, where we will not be seen or bothered." Sloane could see outlines of rocks, and where the road forked, one branch ran close to the coast, the other veered inland slightly.

"Which way, boy?"

Chullain walked into the coastline branch and snuffled around for a while, then went to the inland road and headed down the middle of it; he had chosen. Sloane hitched her bag and followed.

Fifty-two—Little Man under a Bridge

It was almost light with half a sun climbing over the horizon when they came to a bridge crossing a slow gurgling stream lazily making its way to the sea.

"Let's look under the bridge. Maybe we can shelter there?" Sloane asked.

She slid down the steep bank holding onto timbers and stones of the bridge. Chullain was off investigating something else, and Sloane found herself alone, facing a man half her size. A very angry little man.

"Go back!—Go back!—I don't want to hurt you," he shouted, slapping his cudgel against his hand. The stick slapping against his palm punctuating his words.

"I am Sloane.—I mean you no harm.—I am sorry if I frightened you," Sloane said, looking around for Chullain.

"Frighten Stofer?—You frighten Stofer? Stofer is not frightened of a pretty boy." Stofer, feeling much braver now, took two steps closer to Sloane.

Then Chullain announced his arrival, leaping down the embankment, his lips pulled back and baring those ferocious teeth that had killed before and a low growl rumbling in his throat.

Stofer blanched. His large nose and ears remained very red, though, "Now Stofer frightened. Please don't let him eat me. Please!"

Chullain advanced on the terrified little man, his eyes slitty and ferocious. They were level with Stofer's, whose eyes were ready to burst.

"Down, Chullain. Stofer means us no harm. He was just about to offer us shelter for the day."

"Yes! Yes. Welcome. Are there more of you?—I hope not. My place is not large.—Come, come follow me." Stofer seemed to relax as if seeing a way out of his predicament.

"Give me your cudgel first," Sloane said, holding out her hand. Stofer moved to hand it to her. Chullain snarled ominously and Stofer dropped his club.

"Take it! Take it, just don't let him eat me." He was thoroughly terrified again.

"Chullain won't eat you unless you do something to make him. Show us where we can stay for a few hours of rest."

Stofer, turning and, fearfully looking back at Chullain, moved between two huge support timbers stopping in front of a large natural piece of granite that was used as base support in the construction of the bridge.

Stofer turned; slyness was again easing its way across his rather comic features. "I need my cudgel. Sometimes there are many uses for one thing.—And you, boy, will learn that things are not always what they seem."

Sloane silently handed him his cudgel. *You are so right, Stofer, this boy has a lot to learn about things that are not what they seem.*

Stofer tensed at the rumble from Chullain and looked at Sloane.

"Just watch him, boy. Eat him only if you have to," Sloane said. She was starting to enjoy this challenge this funny little man was throwing down.

Stofer, watching the huge furry animal that threatened him missed the small hole in a now visible seam in the granite the first time. But the second time, the cudgel slipped in halfway. Stofer turned; his homely face was alight with pride at what was going to happen.

"Everything is not as it seems.—It seems," he said; he was enjoying himself now. He had to stand on his toes to push up on the cudgel, and when the cudgel could go no further, the granite separated in the middle, at a seam, opening into a dimly lit room.

"Chullain, you go in first. Stofer, you follow

Chullain." Sloane was taking no chances on this sly little man.

Chullain stuck his head through the opening, sampling the air. Then he took several more steps, still sampling the air and twitching his ears for sounds.

"Go on, Stofer. Follow Chullain."

Stofer looked over his shoulder at Sloane. "You're not going to hurt me, are you?"

"Not if you behave. Now get on in there," Sloane said in her new boy's voice.

Stofer stepped quickly through the opening. Chullain was sitting in the middle of the room looking at the dim corner intently. He was not growling.

"How do you see in here, Stofer? Are there torches?"

"Heh, he, he," the little man laughed. "Everything is not as it seems," he said. He then clapped twice real loud. First the floor started glowing pinkly then green, shading into orange and finally a soft white. Then the walls followed, and soon the illumination revealed the room and its contents.

The corner that Chullain was intent on contained a cage, and inside the cage was a frightened little boy.

Sloane rushed to the cage. "Chullain, eat him if he moves," she said. She knelt at the door. It was locked.

"Unlock this!" she ordered.

Stofer, now quaking and quivering, fished a key from his belt pouch and gingerly handed to Sloane as Chullain watched him, lip pulled back over murderous teeth.

"Don't let him eat me." His knees buckled and Chullain was on him.

"No! Not yet!" Sloane shouted. She picked up the large key that Stofer had dropped and unlocked the cage. The boy backed into the corner, looking wildly past Sloane to the opened door behind her.

Sloane stopped her advance, backed slowly out of the cramped cage, and squatted down.

"Come out. It is all right. I won't hurt you. Are you hungry?" The soft words tumbled from her, and the boy's eyes registered that this was not as threatening as before.

He crouch-crawled to the door. He squatted there, looking at Sloane, then at the great Chullain who was standing over a petrified Stofer.

"I-I-I w-wa-want t-to go home."

"I'll take you home. I won't hurt you." Sloane held her arms out, and the little boy rushed part way to her, stopped, and looked into Sloane's face again. Then he hurled himself into her arms, sobbing now.

Sloane held him, crooning and patting him like his mother would have.

He stopped crying, leaned back, and squeezed Sloane's right breast, "You're a woman."

"Yes, and you do not touch a woman there unless asked," Sloane said, removing his little hand. "How long have you been in that cage? What are you called?"

"Torin. I do not know how long. I have eaten three times," Torin said. "I am hungry now."

"Let him up, Chullain, but watch him close. Eat him if he needs it," Sloane said, taking Torin's hand and standing in front of Stofer.

Stofer stood fearfully. "You're a woman?"

"Everything is not as it seems.—It seems." Sloane said, throwing his words back at him. "How long have you had Torin penned up? Get him, get us all some food.—Where did you get him?"

"He stole me off of the bridge when I looked over," Torin said.

"That's not true," Stofer said, he had moved to a cupboard and was getting a roast bird, bread, and a pitcher of milk and setting them on the small table near the cupboard. "He came snooping around under the bridge and saw the Granite open, so I had to take him to protect my secret."

"Go eat." Sloane gave Torin a little nudge, and he ran to the table and ripped a leg off the bird.

"Manners! Eat as if your mother was sitting across from you. Give Chullain some of the bird too." Chullain heard his name and circled the table so he could still watch Stofer and eat. Torin ripped the other leg off and threw it to Chullain, who caught it with an audible snap of his big teeth. Stofer winced when he heard them click.

"Torin, don't you know how to behave? Don't you have any manners?" Sloane said. She smiled because Torin made her think of another messy boy only slightly older.

"I wonder where you are, Merle?" she said, memories of the boy and the *Caoimhe* fresh in her mind.

"My name is Torin I told you, and I'm right here."

"Yes, you are, aren't you?"

Stofer started to edge away from the conversation, but the low growl from Chullain stopped him.

"No, you don't! Stay right there!—What were you going to do with the boy?—No, that doesn't matter yet. Who are his parents?—Why aren't they hunting for him?" Sloane left Torin and advanced on Stofer.

Stofer backed away; he put his hands up to ward off the blows. But none came. He looked around his hands questioning.

"I'm not going to beat you. I want answers."

"I sell the children. I sell them to the Skirniri," Stofer said. His voice cracked and he fell to his knees.

"Then you know what the Skirniri do with them." Sloane's voice was ice. Chullain had never heard that tone from his beloved mistress. His hackles rose, great slobbers ran from his jaws as he advanced on Stofer.

"No, Chullain. We'll not kill Stofer; he will do that himself." Again Sloane was cold as the icy wind off the blue glaciers.

"Torin, do you know the way to your home?" Her voice was soft and caressed the little boy with love.

"I would know it if I saw it. I know which way we came from," Torin said. "Can I have more to eat? I am still hungry."

"Yes. Give Chullain more too.—Stofer, get in the cage until I figure out what to do with you."

Stofer moved reluctantly to the cage holding onto the door before ducking in. "I will be no problem. I give you my word."

"Get in." The icy hardness of the voice caused him to leap into the cage, banging his head and falling to his knees.

"Oh! Am I bleeding? My skull is cracked," he moaned.

No one listened to him. Sloane sat down with Torin at the small table. She ate, while gently asking Torin about his home and family.

Chullain padded over and lay down in front of Stofer's cage. He watched the little man and yawned often, showing large yellowing teeth. Stofer was trembling uncontrollably, but all the while, his eyes searched for escape.

"No escape, Stofer, you have to atone for the children you have doomed to the Skirniri." Sloane unlocked the cage door and stepped back.

Stofer felt soul-shaking fear as he had never felt before. He had only seen it on the face of the children when he handed them over to the loathsome Skirniri. Sloane was implacable; she had never felt the coldness and weight of delivering justice. She did not like what she had to do, but that is the way of justice; it is delivered reluctantly by gentle people; but it is delivered.

"You can feed yourself in this place?" she asked the trembling Troll.

Immediately Stofer perked up; he saw a way out. "Yes, yes, I can stay here for a long time." But he lied; they had eaten the last of the food.

"How do you open the granite from the inside?"

The slyness swept over the despicable creature in a wave of subservience. "It opens the same way with a lever or my cudgel."

"Gather them up for me, every one. Chullain, you make sure he brings every one."

Stofer scurried around the room; he brought back a walking stick. "This is all; you have my other one." He stood with relief mingling with his deceit.

"Where?" Sloane asked motioning with the cudgel.

Stofer went to the wall they had entered and pointed to a hole head high on him.

Sloane gave the cudgel to Stofer and said, "Open it.—Chullain, eat him if he runs."

Stofer, trembling violently, pushed the stick in the hole pushing it up. The granite separated smoothly with sunlight streaming in.

Torin ran out the opening as soon as it was large enough, and he kept running.

"Get back in the middle of the room, Stofer," Sloane said.

Stofer cast a furtive look at freedom, but the growl convinced him of the proper thing to do. He moved to the center of the room and stood.

"Turn around look the other way." Sloane removed her shawl of invisibility when he was facing the opposite wall. She hung it over the lever, pushed the lever down, and when the granite started closing, she slipped outside. The lever still in its slot, but invisible to Stofer.

The room went dark. Stofer clapped his hands like before. Nothing happened. He was sealed in blackness. He ran around the room shrieking, but all was black as his heart. The realization that he was doomed to starving in the coldness of his soul struck him. He heard someone wail, it sounded a lot like some of the children he once heard when he stayed too long with the Skirniri.

"It's me!" he wailed.

Sloane stood silently, scratching Chullain's ears when the tormented shriek whispered its way through the rock. Chullain's ears perked, and he looked at his beloved mistress.

Sloane looked around for Torin, she didn't see him. "It's time to find Torin," she said starting up the embankment. Soon she wouldn't hear the shuddering shrieks coming from the rocks, but others would hear them for hundreds of years.

Fifty-three—The Funeral Pyre

Sloane and Chullain stood at the edge of the bridge and road, searching for Torin. Down the road in the direction they had come, Torin was a small speck running. "It looks like he knows where he is going. He is going to be all right. . . . But I am wondering about those horsemen?"

Sloane was gazing intently at a fast-moving dust cloud in the direction they intended to travel. The figures grew more distinct; it was the small Norse ponies of a Viking foraging party.

The first rider drew abreast of Sloane and looked appraisingly over her. Then he hauled the pony back so violently it went to its haunches. Chullain's deep fierce growls of warning rumbling from his throat stepped between Sloane and the fierce braided-haired Viking. The Viking took his eyes off of Sloane, fastening them on Chullain, the only threat he saw. But he talked to Sloane. "Are you a pretty boy or are you a maid?"

He reached back over his right shoulder and drew a fighting ax, still talking softly to Sloane, but his eyes never left the snarling, dripping, tooth-bared threat between them. "I am Karl the Ax. Your dog is brave but very dead."

Chullain sprang, yellowed teeth dripping, red gums gleaming—**Thuuunk!** The great dog dropped. Karl casually gave his ax hand a twist and lifted the blade clear of Sloane's noble friend's great head.

Sloane felt her heart wrench to a halt, then to a galloping rage. This was her second dog killed by a man. She fixed her gaze on the man walking to her, cleaning the smears off his ax, he returned it to the scabbard on his back.

Karl slowed and stopped several paces from the boy-girl figure standing in front of him. Her eyes bored through him, seeming to change in color and intensity. He felt odd. He felt remorse. He felt her rage, and her sorrow at the loss of her friend. He said nothing. He was a warrior. Death was what he dealt in.

"I must bury him," Sloane said.

"No, we will take him with us and he will have his funeral with Ivar, War Chieftain of Ice Island, who was my father. You will burn with your dog on the fire ship, a sacrifice to accompany Ivar to Vall Halla."

Sloane met Karl's gaze steady and unafraid. "That will do. Treat Chullain as a honored foe." She held out her hands to be bound.

Karl never took his eyes from hers, "Bind her," he ordered.

Sloane was bound, moved to a group of young women, and was tied to the last one.

Karl watched her as she walked. "You are woman. What are you called?"

"My name is of no importance. My friend whom you killed was Chullain."

"Carry the dog on a shield," Karl ordered. He mounted his small horse and cantered off, his mind on the unnamed woman. Tied last in a line of sacrifices for the funeral fire ship of his father Ivar war chieftain.

Sloane trudged gray dust coating her legs and powdering her hair and face. She mourned her friend Chullain, who died as he had lived for her. She did not fear the funeral pyre; she knew she was not destined to die yet.

*　　*　　*

Cillian lazed in the sun. He was pleasantly warm and feeling the urgency mounting for the want of a woman. The small cask of foreign liquor was almost gone, and when it was, he was going to find one, maybe two more.

Cillian had been watching the dust of Karl's party as it approached the camp where all except he was preparing for the funeral of Ivar.

Karl nodded when he drew abreast of Cillian lying on his back, head resting on his helm, drinking horn in his hand.

Cillian didn't acknowledge Karl. He felt that he

would have to kill him one day anyway, so it was a waste of time to even treat him as if he lived.

Karl felt a fear of this quiet deadly mercenary, whom his father had hired. Something would have to happen to this Cillian after the funeral. Cillian was not going to sail with Karl.

Two warriors strode by, bearing a shield with a fallen warrior covered by a dark woolen cape hiding all evidence as to whom, only that there was a body under it.

Then fourteen female captives for the funeral fire ship followed, they hung their heads, their feet dragging in the dust; they had given up all hope.

Cillian examined each as they passed. He had settled on one who reminded him of the girl who haunted him, then the last one caught his attention.

He, no, it was a she. She walked with the confidence of a warrior not afraid of death. She looked at everything she passed as if looking for an escape. Her hair was short and brownish, rather raggedy, but it crowned a face that that made him look again.

"You!—Yes, you. Come here," he said. The words were thick and slurry from the liqueur.

She stopped and the line of captives stopped. For an instance her gaze held his and Cillian felt the pull of the ginger-haired one. But this was not she.

"Leave be, Mercenary! These are for Ivar's fire ship, not for your pleasure." The Norse guard hissed and started the line moving again.

Sloane held Cillian's gaze until she passed him. He stood now jamming his long nose-guarded helm on his head and girding his fighting ax and long sword on. He shook off the languor of the liqueur and followed the party of captives. When they reached the bathhouse, the guards moved among the captives, untying them so they could be cleaned and purified for the trip to Vall Halla.

Cillian moved in and stood in front of the last captive. The one who also held him captive. "Ssshh, come with me," he said, cutting her bonds and taking her hand pulling her around the corner of the bathhouse.

Sloane knew Cillian; she knew he was her only chance of escape, and she knew he did not recognize her. She followed, throwing off the remains of her tethering rope.

No alarm was raised yet. Cillian, still holding her hand, pulled her up close. "Walk behind me like a servant until we get out of camp."

Sloane said nothing, just dropped back two paces and followed. She looked for an avenue of escape and saw several, but something kept her with this man of her dreams and visions. *Why am I staying with this man?*

They cleared the encampment, Cillian slowed, with Sloane falling in step beside him. No words passed between them. Sloane read Cillian, he felt her in his thoughts, and it made him uneasy. If he hadn't been Cillian, he would have even thought he was fearful.

"I need a drink," he announced.

"There is water in the stream," Sloane said.

"It is not water I thirst for," Cillian said.

"I know," Sloane said.

"Who are you?"

"Who do you think I am?" Sloane asked.

"I know not, but you are familiar.—Remain as my serving boy. There is an inn ahead; we will lodge there tonight." Cillian bending down, holding her face in his hands. He removed his hands in a caress across her cheek that sent a shiver through Sloane.

Fifty-four—The Inn

The inn was a crossroads where merchants and Norse raiders traded and bought and sold goods taken in raids for provisions to raid again. Cillian was known here and welcomed as a free spender and good customer.

"Welcome, Raider. When did you start traveling with a pretty boy? Do you not want a woman for the night?"

Sloane heard the voice but could not see the speaker. The voice was high-pitched almost to a point of pain to hear.

"He is a new body servant for me. No women this night, but send me a pitcher of Tuscan wine. To my usual room." Cillian growled, a little embarrassed at the reference to traveling with a pretty boy.

"There is a merchant from the land of yellow men in your room," The high-pitched voice answered.

"Find another one for him quick because he is on his way out. Send up new sheets with the wine. I'll not sleep where a yellow man has lain."

Sloane stepped clear of Cillian; she had to see where this painful voice was coming from.

"Oh," came involuntarily from her. The originator of the voice was a large-breasted bald man with a hairy face like a monkey and a single eye that gleamed black and shiny at her.

"Ahh, maybe the pretty boy is not a boy at all. I am Simian of the tree clan, and you are?" The voice pierced her, but the single eye bored into her. Sloane felt her psyche being searched. She immediately sealed herself the way she had been taught.

Simian felt the wall, and he knew this was no serving boy. "Come with me boy, I'll give you bedding and wine to bring to your master's room."

Then Simian recoiled. He felt the strong probe on his psyche reading his innermost thoughts. "Go. I'll serve you myself. Go."

Cillian was already going up the ladder to his room in the loft. Sloane, hurrying after him, heard the yell and thump as Cillian threw the Chinaman out of the loft to the floor below. Then she heard the strange whimpering of the hurt man.

Cillian threw his helm off, his ax and swords followed. Sloane gathered them up and hung them from pegs in the wall.

"Get the wine!" Cillian was feeling unsure of himself and when that happened, he became a bully.

Sloane met Simian at the ladder. Simian's one eye acknowledged Sloane as the stronger, and he opened wide all that he knew he could not hide anyway. Sloane read him and found no evil. She put her hand on his baldpate, and he lowered his head in salute to a priestess of the Goddess.

"Are you well? Do you require assistance?" he asked.

"No. I am where I am supposed to be for now," Sloane answered.

Sloane took the bedding and the large pitcher of yellow wine from him and delivered them to Cillian.

Cillian put the pitcher to his lips and drank half of it before setting it down. "Change the bed and get in it," he ordered.

Sloane stood in the middle of the room; she looked at Cillian and felt the love she had for this man. She felt it, knowing he did not know her as his ginger-haired vision. Sloane knew what was coming; she did not want it, but she would not stop it.

Cillian tilted the pitcher up to finish it, and Sloane

pulled her jerkin over her head and naked, she slipped into the sleeping pallet.

Cillian went to the ladder and pulled it up so no one could get to his loft room.

Sloane watched as he threw the rest of his clothes off as he walked to her and the sleeping pallet.

She lay passive as he slid in beside her, she knew what was going to happen and as his lips found hers, she felt the liquid heat wash over her. Sloane felt his mouth tender instead of insistent, and she responded until the tenderness was insistent. The moment seized both of them, Sloane her first experience of love and Cillian many times with women, but nothing like this. Sloane felt it when it happened, she knew as she lay with a silken sheen of perspiration hers and Cillian's covering her. She knew she had a new life inside her.

She sent a sleep until morning message to Cillian and left the sleeping pallet pulling on her tunic as she went. She put the ladder down and slipped down the rungs. Simian stood at the bottom; he handed her a small pouch of money and her medicine bag, his one eye showing the concern he felt for her.

"Do not worry for me, Simian. I travel to Norns; there my daughter will be born."

*   *   *

The morning sun had crested and it was midday before Cillian woke from the deep sleep sent him by Sloane. He lay his eyes wide, not moving, the last night's events sliding across his mind. Who was this woman? Where was she? *I don't even know her name!*

Cillian sprang up from the sleeping pallet, searching for the maiden who had shared it with him. *She gave me her first love. But then I took it, didn't I?* He pulled on his jerkin and leggings, jammed his helm on and started for the ladder when he noticed the one eye of Simian watching him.

"Where is she?" Cillian demanded.

"You will never know. I came up here to kill you in your sleep, but I see you have more concern for her than anyone I have ever seen you care for." Simian handed Cillian his own ax that he held.

"You were going to kill me with my ax."

"Go back to your camp, forget this night if you can," Simian said and his head slipped below the loft floor as he descended the ladder.

"Tell me—" Cillian called after him.

"No more, Cillian. You are not welcome here! Leave now."

Cillian finished dressing and left the Inn. He walked by Simian and the single eye followed him out, and he felt it all the way back to the Viking camp.

Ivar's funeral ship was still smoldering thin smoke trails, streaming skyward when Cillian walked back into the camp.

The camp was still sleeping off the drink from the funeral. When the fleet finally sailed, Cillian commanded. Karl had his funeral fire ship like his father, only not so grand.

Cillian stood at the Serpent's Head, the wind pushing the long boat with the mast straining to hold the load of wind the sail had. The bow wake was white and high, the spray being flung back wetting his face, his thoughts drifting from the unknown to the ginger-haired vision that haunted him. The unknown became a dream that didn't happen. But he never had the vivid visions and visitations of his ginger hair again either. He only had dreams that became faded and nebulous as the years passed. He raided and warred, feared from the hot sun sands to the smoking mountains and green-tree massed land to the blue-iced north. He was Cillian the Raider.

*   *   *

Sloane kept off the roads; she crossed a field of millet, then slipped into a loosely wooded area, always in the direction of Norns. Her thoughts were back in the Viking camp and with the young Viking who took from her the last of her childhood and gave her the fruits of womanhood. She knew life stirred in her womb. The thoughts of raising a child did not frighten her. Women raised children by themselves all the time.

What of Cillian? How can I love him when I do not want to stay with him? *I miss Chullain!*

When night fell Sloane lay down where she was and slept dreamless and cold. The morning came late because clouds hid the sun and the rain came in drizzling sheets with the wind that came from all directions.

"I am totally miserable," she said aloud.

I have been miserable before, and it didn't stop me. I have no time to feel sorry for myself. I must find shelter. She stood tall as she could looking in all directions looking for some kind of shelter.

There! A whisper trail of smoke drifted up off the path from deeper in the forest of conifers and aspens. Sloane lowered her head and headed into the wind-driven drizzle heading to the source of the smoke. Her hair was slowly growing, and the stain was wearing out of it. She fingered the strands as she walked. *I will never be the same, will I?* She questioned the wind and the rain.

Then thoroughly soaked and shivering with the cold, she approached a small neat cottage. A green door stood closed, and the smell of warmth and food filtered around it making her almost giddy, if she had not been Sloane.

As she raised her hand to tap on the door, it swung open.

"Come in. I have been waiting for you." Gwen of the Glen Faeries held out her arms and pulled Sloane in.

Silent tears flooded Sloane as she burrowed into the embrace of love.

This is the start of the end of Sloane's story as told by her.

The rest of her story will be told by Cillian the Raider.

Cillian's Story

My Story

This is my story. I start in battle, but the battle is unimportant. What is important is Sloane. I speak as a warrior and slayer of men. My kind has many women but few loves. This is my story and my love for one woman; Sloane.

Fifty-five—Ginger Hair

I saw her as my blood lust was receding; the village warriors were all down, only the infirm, the old, and women left cowering. There were no more worthy opponents.

She stood next to an unusual shrine, her arm around another young female. She was afraid but would not cringe. Her hair glowed Ginger Fire in the setting sun.

"UUUUURRRRAAAAAHHH!" The killing cry rang from behind me, and Ogurr lumbered past still in his berserker rage, intent on the women.

As he passed in front, I clove him from neck to armpit. I would have had to kill him sometime anyway. No one but me would have this woman.

Eyes of color I know not how to say looked at me over the body of Ogurr. No words passed, but when I turned and left the carnage, she followed with the smaller female, as I would have ordered.

We wound our way through the smoldering, screaming, burning village of Norns, past rape and murders, and looting still in progress. I motioned for them to walk in front of me, she moved there, sheltering the other as if she read my mind.

We waded to my long boat, where she boosted the girl over the gunnels.

"Now me, Raider," she said, and put both hands on my shoulders and stepped on my hip bone, leaping over

161

the side. Her legs and bottom bared to the setting sun but for a instant.

"You'll bump that pretty little bottom for me to-night." I leaped over the gunnels to take her.

"Raider, not now. Casidhea has a wound." She pulled the rough shift up, revealing mangled flesh where one of our hounds had been. This Casidhea turned soulful eyes on me, but cried not.

"Balder, come out, you old rascal," I hollered.

From a pile of furs and canvas, a simple smiling face emerged. "You need me, Cillian?"

"Get your medicines and repair the girl's wound."

Ginger Hair examined the man to whom she was to trust. "Give me the bag. I'll do the healing."

They worked together repairing Casidhea's wounds. The sound of pillage was fading with the fading light. I raised the anchor stone and used the night breeze to anchor again several miles from the burning village.

Balder was a renowned healer, but the Ginger Hair was working from his medicine bag as if it were hers.

The halyards were soft slapping in the night breeze; a lone seabird flew silent across the face of the moon. Our gods were satisfied this night. The villager's gods must have fled.

"They are false gods, Raider." Ginger Hair was standing beside me.

"How goes the girl Casidhea?" *How did she know what I was thinking?*

"She will heal. Your Balder has good medicines," she said.

I reached out; she did not flinch and raised her chin to my fingers. I tilted her little face up and to the side, searching for the difference that was drawing me in.

"What are you called?"

"Sloane," she answered.

"Do you know why I saved you?" I asked, not entirely sure I knew.

"Yes."

Then silence as I tried to fathom this woman. She returned gaze for gaze.

"I can take you right now."

"Yes," she answered.

"I can inflict great pain on you."

She answered with silence.

"I can kill you and throw your body into the Irish Sea."

"Raider, all these things have been done me, except the killing. Do what you must. Only you will do none of these." She removed her face from my hands. "Wash yourself Raider. You have the stink of slaughter." Sloane moved to the step behind the Serpents Head, threw her arms wide, and breathed deep the night air.

Framed by the moon, she appeared to lose form for a instant. *I must be seeing things.*

I threw off my jerkin and plunged into the cold dark sea, washing this night's killing from my body. When I clambered back aboard, she was curled up with Casidhea in her arms.

I joined Balder at the tiller seat. "Ketill, Grimr, Ogurr, and Ulfr aren't going to be happy with you moving the ship," he said, handing me the drinking horn.

"I killed Ogurr this night," I said, quaffing deeply.

"You would have had to sometime anyway. Better now. This Sloane . . . why did you bring her?—You never brought a woman back before." Balder questioned me with the love of a father.

"I don't know, old man, I was searching for another kill. The rage was gone when I saw her. She stood protecting the little one, Casidhea. Then nothing but her mattered. That is when I slew Ogurr." I handed the drinking horn back to him.

"She cast a spell on you," was all he said, "Go to bed, we will have problems in the morning when the crew finds us."

I sat up watching Sloane sleep. The wind changed and blew in off the ice pack of the north and it got cold. I knelt and was putting a bearskin over them when Sloane's eyes opened inches from mine. She had no fear; I saw only wisdom, compassion, and strength in them. *Why do I wait?*

"Go to sleep, Cillian, all will be revealed in its time," she said and pulled the skin snug and with a little snore was sound asleep again.

She used my name. She didn't call me Raider. I drifted off into the same troubled dream riding, sailing and walking, always searching, searching for what?

Fifty-six—Steer to the Blue Star

The sound of a small boat bumping alongside the long boat woke us all. "Cillian, you're a dead man," came roaring up from the boat with eight rowers and the tiller man who was doing the shouting.

When Grimr stuck his filthy, blonde-braided head over the gunnels, I split it with my ax, and he fell back in the boat.

"Come aboard, but Cillian is not doing the dying today," I said. They straggled on board, the fight gone. Einarr slit Grimr's belly so he would sink and let him into the sea.

"Cillian has some playthings on board. I take the little one," Ketill said, stepping over the sleeping pallet to get Casidhea. I took up my throwing ax, but Ketill had stopped, he turned to us, gurgling his last words. He was dead before he hit the deck.

Sloane and Casidhea turned from the still-twitching corpse and joined Balder at the tiller.

Raiders understand violent sudden death. But this——a chill shuddered through us all.

"She, they are mine," I roared, but I fear it was not much of a roar.

Sloane smiled a tight little knowing smile at me over the head of the soulful-eyed Casidhea.

Balder made room and Casidhea sat beside him; Sloane stepped over Ketill and stood beside me. "Set the sail, Raider, we are being pursued," she said and pointed to three masts breaking the horizon.

All eyes followed her pointing arm and for all their barbarity, what was left of my crew were sailors. Ketill's belly was opened and he was tossed, the sail hoisted and the seven remaining set to on the oars.

"Who is it, Sloane?" Somehow it seemed natural to ask of her what I did not know.

"Haarald, he collected tribute from the village four days ago; that is why you found no treasure." She stood beside me with sailor's legs already, her hair blowing and whipping my jerkin with a flicking noise that only I heard.

I bent and said, "You're mine."

She said nothing but her little smile opened and her teeth glistened through.

"They are slow; they will not catch *Aoife,*" Balder shouted above the wind. "Look, Cillian, look who is your helmsman."

Little Casidhea stood, her bandaged leg braced against Balder, the tiller held with both hands. Her face stern with concentration until she noticed Sloane watching, then the little-girl laughter mixed with the wind and softened all our hearts.

"Ship oars, we'll run with the wind," I shouted. The deck quivered, the mast moved back with the pressure of wind and the *Aoife* flew across the waves. The cold spray was wetting us all, but the freedom of the moment was all that mattered.

We sailed through the night; I took the tiller and Sloane sat beside me. Casidhea and Balder slept at our feet. We did no talking, but somehow I knew she was learning of me, while I fell deeper under her spell. When the moon was directly over the mast, she took the tiller and set *Aoife's* Serpent Head to follow a new star I had not seen before this night.

"Steer to the Blue Star, Cillian, that way lies our future." And she stood, pulled her cloak tight, and lay beside Casidhea and Balder at my feet.

I didn't care if I slept. If I'm awake, I don't dream. I don't like searching for I know not what.

Balder sat up, looked at the stars, and jumped up. "Where? Cillian."

"The Blue Star, we steer to the blue star," I said.

"Oh, well, it is a long way from the monastery on the Green Isle. Do you remember the monastery?" Balder peered at me, and I could see him as he was then in his monk's habit. When I was eight, Ogurr's father, Gunnarr, sacked the monastery, killing all save the Monk Balder and me. He brought us back to his fjord home as companion and teacher for Ogurr, his eldest son.

"Yes, Father. I remember. I was training to be a monk like you." I leaned back and listened to the hiss of the hull and the whispering of the canvas, as Balder took the helm. "The Blue Star, old friend. The blue star that is our future now." I drifted off to sleep with Sloane's image etched in my psyche.

There were no searching dreams this night, only visions of Sloane. She was beckoning me to join her, but all was fuzzy around and behind her.

Seven nights we followed the blue star. During the day a fish with a nose and teeth guided us by swimming at *Aoife*'s bow. I had removed the serpent's head because we were traveling in peace. Sloane was leaning over the bow as if conversing with the fish; her shift had pulled up, revealing a creamy expanse of roundness that was causing my crew to grow restless. For some reason I did nothing but look and lust, no better than my crew.

Balder left the tiller to Casidhea, stepping over Einarr, Ulfr, Brundr, and Torfi, smacking their heads with his dirk hilt as he passed. He stopped behind Sloane, shielding her bottom from view, and handed her something green.

When he returned, he lumped the rest of the crew's head that he missed on the way forward, and he gave me a look that said, *you need one too.*

Sloane, unconcerned for our scrutiny, pulled on the green trews. I recognized them as being the ones I had worn when Gunnarr took us so long ago. I wonder what else Balder still has from those long-ago years?

I felt a tug and looked down. Casidhea looked up at me. I did not know if she could speak, we had only heard her laugh. "You were not always as you are, and you will not remain as you are." The little slightly triangular face smiled shyly, and she returned to sit with Balder.

She doesn't know. Balder probably told her something.

"Casidhea has not heard of you from Balder. I told her of your past," Sloane said.

I did not see her come aft, and I was startled but pleased to see her close. "But I have told you nothing of my life," I protested.

Sloane laid her hand on my forearm, "We make land fall when the sun sets. This is a special place."

"But there are no birds, the sea is clear and deep. I smell no land."

"Nevertheless we will make land fall, and the first night must be spent on the *Aoife,* Cillian." Sloane squeezed to emphasize.

"When did we reverse roles and you take command?" I asked.

"The roles are the same, you are just wiser. We will need your strength before we leave this land." Sloane stepped close. I could feel her body warmth; she enveloped my senses.

"Are you a Witch?"

"No, just a woman and mother," she said, "And you command, Cillian, you."

She made me want to think I commanded, but I had never commanded before taking orders and course changes from a man, let alone a woman.

"Land, land," Snorri shouted. He was sitting at the masthead ordered there after Sloane told me we would strike land.

Fifty-seven—Island of Women

Against a blood red orb of a setting sun, the black smudge grew larger and the sun sank out of sight behind it. We furled sail and set to on the oars; each man had his weapons beside him, as Balder steered us into a protected cove. There was no beach, just rock cliff covered with strange trees and hanging vines.

"Drop the anchor stone well away from the cliffs," I ordered. Einarr gave the signal to the rowers and they back watered, The *Aoife* slowed, stopped, and the anchor went over.

"Why do we not make land our bed tonight?" I asked Sloane.

"Those who live there will watch and decide if they will allow us to come ashore," she answered; she was beautiful with moonlight caressing her face.

"I never ask permission to come ashore. . . ."

Sloane cut me off. "This time you will or we will all perish."

The night, dark as heart blood, sucked us in. The sound of the sea against *Aoife's* hull could not be heard, there were no bird sounds. I spoke, "Sloane, Sloane." But I could not hear my voice.

Fear choked me; I had never felt this kind of terror, I screamed with no sound, my heart raced to exploding, my breath was gone. I was dying. Then it subsided and I heard the slap of the sea, the moonlight again spread its magic on us. I looked on the faces of the crew and saw they had felt what I had.

"What was that, Sloane?" I asked.

Sloane and Casidhea were standing in the bow, the moon bathing them in light other than what was illuminating us.

"You have felt all the terrors and pain you have inflicted upon others. Remember this night. It is yours now to protect and defend those in need."

We all heard this. But it was in our heads.

169

Balder was doing something I hadn't seen since we were taken from the monastery, he was kneeling in prayer to God.

The crew glanced at and then looked away from each other, they were different men; most pulled their cloaks about themselves and slept. Two, only Snorri and Erikr, talked softly about what had happened.

Sloane and Casidhea stood beside me. Little Casidhea took my scarred and murderous hand and said, "You were never as you are now, and you will never be what you were."

I said nothing. I was feeling something I had never felt before, my nose burned, my throat hurt, and my eyes were wet. I turned away into the shadow of the mast; no one must see Cillian weep.

Sloane stepped around the other side of the mast, met me, pulled my head down, and started to kiss me, but I kissed back. I'd waited too long for this.

She gently disengaged both of us, shaken by the kiss, "There's still quite a lot of the raider left in you."

"Now is the time, Sloane." I would not be put off this time. All were asleep now.

"Almost, Cillian, we are close, one more kiss, then we sleep," she said, and we melted into the moonlit shadows.

I did not sleep. I had no wish to search in my dreams, when I could watch what I wanted, sleep curled up with Casidhea. I still wondered, were they sisters, mother and daughter, or what?

Sloane was not like the women I had back at Gunnarr's fjord. You see I grew tired of Gunnarr when I was sixteen, and I slew him and took his wives, all except Ogurr's mother. That is why he followed me, after a fashion. I knew only the women I took after battle or those of

170

my household at Gunnarr's fjord. I had no desire to return to the fjord.

The morning sun revealed a lush grass and tree-lined shore with a beach landing. The beach had no sand or mud; it was of small round moss-covered stones.

"Where are the cliffs?" Balder asked and crossed himself.

Casidhea's laughter, and her hand in his calmed the old priest.

I could see the escort waiting, just as Sloane said they would be. There were several tents and it looked like cooking fires were lit.

"Put us on the beach, Einarr," I ordered and stood in the bow with Sloane, Casidhea, and Balder.

"They are all women," Torfi said.

I dropped Sloane over the bow first. I managed to grasp her bottom and feel the softness of her breast as I did, causing her to smile and her eyes to shine. *I would have her yet.*

"Sloane, do the men come ashore?" I called down to her. She was talking in a warbling tongue to a motherly plump little woman.

The plump little mother looked up and in a booming voice all could hear said. "Everyone come, we have food and baths, bring everything that requires cleaning and repair." She held out her arms as if to embrace the *Aoife*.

The men gave out a shout and spilled over the gunnels, splashing towards shore. Before I could enforce ship's discipline, the loud-voiced little mothers checked their momentum with "Deposit your weapons in the first tent, eat in the second."

The men did something they never did for me; they formed a line behind Einarr and filed into the first tent and exited without weapons.

171

"That has got to be a first," Balder said. "What magic are we in?"

I walked ashore alone as Sloane was now standing in a circle of women. What was going on I don't know or want to know. I walked past the weapons tent but did not leave any of my tools of the trade. I was Cillian, Raider. Whatever might have happened last night did not change the fact that I was a Warrior. I was different now, but I was still Cillian, but maybe not a raider any more.

Fifty-eight—Feast and Journey Inland

"Cillian, won't you leave all but your throwing ax. For me, Cillian," Casidhea pleaded. She stood with another young female; they had pleasant but determined looks.

"Please, Cillian."

I slipped off the long sword, the short sword, and the dagger, and handed the long sword and dagger to Casidhea the short sword to the other girl.

Casidhea said, "Thank you, this is Idun." And they ran into the tent with my weapons. I stood fiddling with my throwing ax until they returned.

"What is this place?" I asked Casidhea, but I searched Idun's face for a clue. Idun's face was young, her body young, but her eyes seemed ageless.

Idun's voice was the musical voice of spring and youth; it charmed me to hear her say. "This is Mother's Island, a place of peace and renewal."

"Whose mother? One of the gods?" I asked.

Idun and Casidhea filled the flower-scented air with the laughter of a brook spilling over pebbles, a warbler throating his song to the morning. I looked at the tent where my crew who only a week ago were murdering and raping, now sat like gentlemen at a table eating with females of all ages surrounding them.

"Come, we eat." Casidhea took my hand and led me to the table. Grizzled old Snorri of two hundred battles smiling a gap-toothed grin in a scarred and bearded face shoved over and made a place for me.

"Eat, Cillian, surely we have chanced upon on an outpost of the gods," Ulfr said, handing me a bowl filled with chunks of reddish somethings. Ulfr, who always scowled, who only laughed when he was killing, smiled, and chuckled like an old grandpa.

"What is this?" I asked. It was delicious.

"Who cares? Eat, eat," Einarr shouted. The childlike exuberance caused the whole tent to laugh.

I felt Sloane. She stood at the tent entrance and motioned me to join her. Casidhea got up with me, and we both joined Sloane outside the tent.

"Cillian, we have a journey inland. You, Casidhea, and me."

"I'll get the men ready," I said. I was glad to have something to do.

Sloane stepped close, "Your crew is not allowed inland, only you. And why will be revealed in the womb."

"What about my men?" I asked. *Womb? Revealed in the womb?*

"Cillian, this island has no men. It is the generational time for some of the women to have children. These women have selected whom they want to father their baby—" Sloane paused, chose her words, then continued. "Your crew of seven men will father all the children on this island for this generation. Once you yourself were a son here, but as with all male babies, you were delivered to a monastery. This island keeps only females."

Me, born here. **NO.** *I remember my mother. I remember her songs.*

"It's true, dear Cillian, you will learn more in the womb. But look, did you ever think you would see your crew like this?" Sloane turned me towards the steaming bath tent.

Einarr led them, shaven, and shorn, scrubbed pink, looking like sheepish little boys except for the weals and whorls of old wounds. Equally radiant young women led my mighty Raider Warriors to individual tents.

"Brundr has four girls," I protested.

"He is the youngest; he will make the best babies," Sloane said, "Are you envious?" She lowered her eyes, and the ginger hair fell off her shoulder as she tilted her head and opened one eye mischievously peeking at me.

"Not if I get you, Sloane," I said, reaching for her. And to my surprise, she let me catch her.

"Run, get us three ponies," she said to Casidhea, who was watching us with interest.

"Yes, Mother," she said and ran off.

"So you are her mother? I thought maybe—. Where is her father?" I asked, feeling the length of her against me, not wanting this talk. "Let's go in one of those tents," I said, pulling her after me.

"Not this way, Raider, we've walked this path before. When the time is right, you will receive better than you give." She kissed me and slipped away.

We walked this path before? Had I known her in my early days of raiding? I knew only women I took. I remember no one I loved. But there was one . . . once, only once I—. I mounted the tiny brush-maned pony, still trying to put the pieces of this puzzle together.

"You will find your answers in the womb," Sloane said.

"How do you know what I am thinking?" I kicked the midget horse into a jolting run. Behind me I heard Casidhea laughing. I must make a ridiculous sight bouncing in this little saddle. I reined the little horse to walk, and they caught up to me.

Fifty-nine—The Womb

We rode silently. I never saw such lush, fertile country, and everything seemed in harmony. *Everything except me.*

"Accept what is offered and you will feel harmonious."

I looked at Sloane, then at Casidhea. Which one said that? They exchanged small quick smiles.

"There is the womb entrance," Casidhea said. "I'll wait here." She dismounted and loosened the cinch on her pony.

"I don't see a womb entrance; all I see is that huge old tree stump," I said.

"Look at the roots," Sloane said.

Two roots ran on the surface of the ground at angles to each other, and where they joined the tree was a large split where lightning must have struck at some time. "I see only that old stump."

"Use your eyes, Raider. Did you never look to see what you were jamming yourself in?" Sloane sounded angry, she had glistening, tear-filled eyes.

I reached for her and she pulled away. "Look at the thighs, look at the vagina, dolt. Go over and squeeze in and crawl until you can go no further."

"Alone?" I was afraid. Cillian the Raider was afraid. I

stepped down. The closer I got to the opening, the more it looked like the life opening gate of a woman. I dropped my ax and slipped my jerkin off. I was naked. I looked back hopefully to where Sloane stood with her arms around Casidhea. Mother and daughter's eyes bored me to my soul. *What did I do to deserve this?*

I had to duck and turn sideways; inside I stood in a small area that was much too big to be part of the stump. I thought it would be dark, but there was a warm pink fuzzy light all around me. I reached out to touch the next entrance and jerked my hand back. It was warm, soft, and silky. *Maybe I should stay here for a while. Then go back out and say I saw nothing.*

"Go until you have to crawl, then crawl until you slide on your belly."

I ducked though the second entrance, the warm silky sides closed in on me. I pushed forward until I had to kneel and crawl. The air I breathed was new, clean, and fresh. I had thought it would be old, dank, moldy. Now I was on my belly, pushing forward with fingers and toes.

My head pushed through into a golden gossamer-lighted round room. The air was now sweet like a new baby or mother's milk. I felt peace, I felt harmony.

"Nial, Nial, come inside and visit your mother."

I wasn't scared. I wasn't Nial. I pushed myself into the round room and when I stood, I stood on air.

"I am Cillian," I said to the beautiful woman who sat on air.

"You were Nial when I birthed you. Nial the champion of My Island." The woman held out her hand to me.

"I am Cillian," I said and took her hand.

"Look at me and remember," she said and sang a lullaby that blew the clouds of Lethe from my mind.

"Do you remember the first time you saw Sloane?"

she asked. I stepped up in space and sat facing my mother. She held out her arms and I was clasped to my mother's breast. "It was not when you sacked Norns."

"If not then, when, Mother?"

"Nine years ago when Chieftain Ivar was sent to Vall Halla. Do you remember stealing one of the sacrificial maids?"

Then I remembered the blazing fires, the drunken warriors, and the young girl. She couldn't have had fifteen years. She was the last of the female sacrifices for Ivar's funeral party. I plucked her from the line, and no one knew. "But she had raven hair, Mother."

"She was traveling to Norns to set up the shrine for *Birth and Renewal*. She blacked her hair to travel through unnoticed, but Ivar's men took her. Now what do you remember?" my mother asked me.

"My mother, I do not want this memory. I love the woman Sloane." I raised my eyes to hers, they were not accusing. They were all knowing.

"The daughter Casidhea is your daughter."

"I ran with the girl for miles to safety, but I got drunk—got drunk. I was young." It was the agony I felt the first night here.

"You put the girl child Casidhea in her womb," my mother said. "Sloane is one of our daughters who must go and administer to the outside. And you are her protector. You have to help her in her mission. I do not know if she will ever let you come to her bed."

"What is her mission? What can I do? Who am I, Cillian or Nial?"

"On my island and with my sisters, you are Nial. In defense and protection of Sloane and Casidhea, you are Cillian." My mother's form began to shimmer and the room dimmed, before it went dark, I heard, "You must help Sloane stop Black Haarald."

When I became aware of my surroundings again, I was standing in an old stump hollowed by Thor's lightning, shivering and naked.

Sixty—Sailing to Norns

When next I opened my eyes, I was on a sleeping pallet in a circular tent, much like the tents my crew were entertaining or being entertained in. I didn't know where Sloane was and did not know how to handle what I now knew. I never imagined being a father, especially of a daughter. Sloane, whom I love. I find I took her by force when she was but a child. *What do I do or say when I do meet them again?*

"You did not force an unwilling girl. I was reluctant, but I was willing." Sloane stood beside my pallet. "Now get up, we must sail before the moon is at its zenith."

"The crew?"

"They are aboard the *Aoife,* calmer, cleaner, and well fed, but with no memory of this island.

"Casidhea, does she know I'm—."

"She knew when you slew Ogurr that you were her father, you were protecting her even then," Sloane said; she stood on tiptoe and pulling my jerkin over my head, her body pushed against me and I folded her in my arms. "No, no, Raider your timing is always off. We must sail to Norns."

I watched her walk to the tent entrance; she still wore my old green trousers, and she wore them well. Her tunic just covered what I coveted. She felt my eyes, and stopped short of the tent entrance, she sagged. In two steps I was at her side and locked her in embrace.

"Help me, Cillian, I do not have the strength by myself." I felt her lips at the base of my throat. That is not all I felt.

"You women don't need me, you didn't even want me. My crew you wanted." I felt her stir and strengthen in my arms; she pushed back against them; her lower body molded against me.

"I need you to be a man. All of life requires the man force. I need you for my pleasure when our task is finished, and my pleasure will be tenfold for you." She breathed into my lips and soul through that kiss, the certainty that I would die for her if need be.

Einarr had the *Aoife* floated, and Balder had seen to the provisioning, we were ready to sail except for us. I lifted Sloane up and as she brushed close, she whispered, "Tenfold."

The moon was near its zenith as we cleared the cove inlet. A loud hissing and a noise like shaking out a blanket caused us to look to the island one last time. The beach was again becoming sheer rock cliffs covered with trees and vines. You say this cannot happen. Friend, does day become night? Does winter freeze summer? This all happened.

"What course, Cillian?" Balder asked.

"Let the wind take her, old friend. Let the wind take her," I said. "Einarr, see to the lashing of the stores, make us seaworthy."

"Do we put the Serpents Head up?" Torfi asked.

I looked at the faces of the crew; they were the faces of good sturdy fighting sailors. We were no longer a crew of raiders. "No, we sail in peace," I said.

Balder had tied the tiller amidships to let the wind

179

put us where it wanted. He motioned me to sit. "I remember and I know what happened on the island. And it is good. We go to a great battle of men and men and spirits and spirits.

"There is only one God, but there are many spirits. My God has welcomed me back." He laid his hand on me and continued, "Sloane of the Ginger Hair and Clever Casidhea are yours. But they belong to the Mysteries of Life and Womanhood. You may enjoy but never control."

I said nothing; there was nothing to say. The woman who bore me a daughter and that daughter stood in the bow. The *Aoife* cut through the water, the hissing hull pushing up a silver mustache across her bow. The wind that was pushing us was not an east, not a west, not a north, nor even a south wind; I believe it was Mother's Wind.

Sixty-one—Black Haarald's Story

We sailed, letting the wind do all the work; the crew ate and slept; and Sloane told us the grim tale of Black Haarald.

Black Haarald was also a son of the Island, his mother Freya fell in love with Od and left the island with him, Haarald was born at Od's fjord. Od was a Mage, a wanderer; across the land and through womanhood. He soon abandoned Freya and Haarald. Destitute Freya sold secrets of the Sisterhood to the Cult of Skirnir to stay alive.

The Skirniri are followers of the Phallus. Their sole purpose is domination of female power, wisdom, influence, and destruction of Mother's Island. The Sisterhood did not trust Freya to her to allow her to return. They changed the location of the island, after sending them to a small fjord to live, supplying them with all they needed.

Freya turned to the black arts. Haarald was an eager disciple, and he became the scourge of the small shrines to the Mother that were located in the scattered Dells and Glens. Haarald became a Skirniri, and through black magic and murder, he became Black Haarald, the High Priest of the Skirniri. Even the Skirniri were afraid of him. His hatred and war against the sisterhood of Mother's Island and her Priestess Emissaries became total. There were no shrines in a thousand leagues, but he had yet to find the way to the Island. Many Priestesses died terrible deaths, not revealing the secret.

"So, Cillian, we have to do what is abhorrent to the sisterhood; we have to destroy Black Haarald. We represent birth and renewal, not destruction," Sloane said.

"But, I—we saw you destroy Ketill when he was going to take Casidhea," I said. The way and the suddenness of his death was still fresh in my mind.

"Destroy Ketill? No. Ketill destroyed himself. The enormity of what he was going to do killed him." Sloane sat earnestly trying to make me understand.

"I don't believe that. I have seen him do much worse," I said.

"Well, he might have seen his daughter in Casidhea," Sloane said. "Some of the sisters do have the power to shape shift, and fade from sight."

"Do you and Casidhea? . . . Yes, yes, you do I've seen you fade." I never realized the power of these women. I did not understand it. But it made sense now; men have all the physical power. But the women have the Meta Physical, the spiritual power.

"Sloane, I have this dream—"

181

She interrupted me. "You are always searching for something."

"Yes. How do you know these things I have told no one?" I asked.

"I have looked into your soul. I accepted you into my body. I nurtured and bore your seed. Now I give you Casidhea, your daughter, she is part of your search." Sloane took my hand, gazing deep into my core; I was immobilized with love, lust, and the whole of everything I did not understand. She continued, "You will be the instrument we use to bring down Black Haarald, You and your crew will be the Sword and Ax for us."

"After—when it's all ov—" I struggled to ask Sloane our future together.

"Cillian, Raider of my heart, we will have time together after there is Peace and Harmony in the land." She held me, Cillian, Scourge of the civilized world, as she would a little boy. *And I didn't care.*

Sixty-two—Love on the *Aoife*

We beached at Norns. I could not believe this was the town we had sacked and burnt. Einarr and the crew unloaded as if they had never seen let alone destroyed the village.

"Balder, do you remember what we did here?" I asked.

"Yes," he answered.

"Einarr, Torfi, Orn, do you remember this place?" I shouted to the unloading party.

"We were here once, it was smaller," Einarr said, and Orn shrugged.

"They do not remember the horror they inflicted," Sloane said from beside me, slipping her arm around me and squeezing.

"I like this," I said and laid my arm across her shoulders. "But why do I remember, and Balder?"

"You have the burden to protect Norns now. You must know what you must not allow. This is a different Norns. The time we spent on the island is not the same as here. Black Haarald is twenty times stronger than he was when you sacked Norns." She swung around, still holding me and faced me. "Tonight on the *Aoife,* tenfold," she said. Her lips, breath, and mouth again seared me.

The *Aoife* was anchored two cables from shore. The small boat bobbed beside her. I was feeling a fear I had never known, and it was of a woman. I searched the shore for another boat; there were none, where at sundown there had been dozens.

I had purchased a new jerkin of finest leather not three hours ago in preparation for this night. The only way to get to Sloane was to swim. I would not shout for her to come get me in the small boat. I stripped there on the shore in the moonlight; I couldn't help feel that something was happening to me.

The water was cold, invigorating. I was into my thighs when I slid forward in a strong one-arm stroke; my other hand held my jerkin and ax out of the water. When I reached the small boat, I tossed clothes and weapon in.

"Leave them there," Sloane's soft red hair hung loose over the side as she spoke.

"But I'm naked," I protested.

"So am I. It is time to learn who you are, and to tell you who I am. Swing up on the anchor rope." She stepped back, I could no longer see her.

I stood naked and dripping in front of Sloane. She dried me and led me to the sleeping area near the helm.

We stood facing each other. I could feel the sexual tension building, but something held it in check. Sloane stood feet slightly apart, not tall, her head just under my shoulder. Her breasts were standing heavy and firm, the nipples slightly erect; she had a small waist with just the suggestion of a tummy, and hips that flared and swelled. This was a woman; this was the one I wanted. But I felt if she ever became mine, it would only be momentary.

"Ah, Cillian, you are the Raider no more. You know one of the truths: you will possess me and I you. And the possession will be fleeting and memorable." She stepped into my arms, and we sank to the skins.

If I told you of the heights and ecstasy attained, you would say I lie, and since this is chronicle of truths, let me give you a comparison. Think back on your most earth-shattering lovemaking. Multiply this by one hundred.

We lay in the moonlight; she traced a deep whorl of scar tissue that ran from my right shoulder to nipple. "Tell me of this," she asked with a kiss.

"A Black Giant in a land of heavy green and stinking black water gave me that. He opened me with a stone ax," I said. Then I sat up, "And you tell me of this." I traced with a soft finger a faint blemish of lightened skin on one breast that migrated to her navel.

"No Cillian, that is not fair; you have no need for this truth." Her eyes glistened with tears, where they had shone with passion.

"Is this not a night in which we learn?"

"Black Haarald dripped hot oil to try and force me to reveal The Island." I gathered her in and held her, and friend, Cillian was crying. But I sent the world notice

184

Black Haarald was a dead man. Cillian was still a warrior.

Eighty leagues away, Black Haarald engaged in an unnatural practice with one of his creatures. He felt a chill as he never felt before. With a curse he rolled the creature from him. "Provision the ships, conscript troops, we sail, we ride, and we march to crush all who follow the Teachings of the Island," he shouted, and the chill caused him to shudder.

Sloane and I lay examining each other's bodies, I noticed other little scars and evidence of being treated rough. I just kissed them and hurt inside; each mark on her body was equal to ten men who would die.

"Cillian, do you know who you are now? Who I am?" She was sitting holding her knees, her hair spilled all around like red gold lace in the moonlight. She held her head at a little angle, looking up at me.

I loved her more than life when I answered, "I am a son of the Mother, I am Nial, champion of the Island. I am the father of Casidhea. I am Cillian, the sword and ax of Sloane. I am the man who loves Sloane." I heard a little sob from her, but I continued. "Sloane is Casidhea's mother. Sloane is Protector of the Natural Way. Sloane is the woman who let me love her twice."

"Three times Cillian, three times." She absorbed me; I floated to a place I'd never visit again. I knew that this was our last time together.

The next morning I rowed us to shore, and we separated, Sloane went to marshal all of nature that could be called upon to fight the plague of Black Haarald and the Skirniri.

185

Sixty-three—Casidhea, My Daughter

Casidhea and I inspected what defenses Norns had. Casidhea was my responsibility now; we accepted the knowledge that Sloane was part of something we weren't.

"Are you going to call me Cillian or Father?" I asked the little grown-up who was my eight-year-old daughter.

Casidhea turned that little face that was so much like Sloane's to me and said. "Father, I shall call you Father. But if I get angry at you, I might call you Raider or Cillian."

I reached down, scooped her out of the pony's saddle, and pulled the little body to my chest. I had to do something; Cillian was about to cry again.

I was buffeted with a feeling as powerful as the feeling of lustful love I had for Sloane. This little person, this little female with red blonde hair; she had seized my heart and made it hers.

"Father, it's not bad to cry. See, I too have tears." And she took my right hand. The hand that slew men by the dozens, and touched it to her tears.

Sloane's voice came on the wind. "Love each other. Care for each other. You are Cillian and Casidhea, family of Sloane."

We rode back into Norns subdued and missing Sloane. Balder and the crew were waiting on the beach.

"Black Haarald with fleet of fifteen long boats are but two days away," Balder said.

Einarr in his simple way said, "We fight."

"There are fifteen long boats, with forty or fifty fighting men in each." As of old I stood in front of my old crew of raiders. But this time Casidhea held my sword hand. "The most we can get from Norns will be about one long boat's worth, including you. We will be about fifty men."

186

Casidhea removed her hand from mine and stepped in front of my old raiders. "We fight!" she shouted. "We fight!"

"We fight," resounded in the inlet. The cliff birds were startled out of their perches and added their cacophony to our. **"We fight."** The seals on the rocks added their barking to the symphony of defiance. **"We fight."** roared out to sea as the villagers added their voices.

*　　*　　*

Two days away in the lead long boat, Black Haarald looked up and cupped his ear. "Did you hear anything?" he asked his perverted creature consort, who dropped to the position he knew would please his master. Black Haarald felt fear. He turned away, wondering if he had really heard a little girl's voice shouting "We Fight" on the winds.

*　　*　　*

Casidhea gathered the women of Norns and taught them healing practices. I was amazed that the women would listen and follow her. She was like a miniature Sloane, moving from group to group, showing this, explaining that. She looked up once, saw me watching, and stuck out her tongue. I had to laugh; it was good having a daughter.

Sixty-four—Black Haarald

Balder gathered the older men into fortification details, and they rebuilt the sea wall where it had tumbled back into the sea. "This won't stop schoolchildren, let alone

Black Haarald's mercenaries," he said. "But it keeps the worriers occupied, and I'm the biggest worrier."

"What about God, old friend? Surely he will help confront all this evil?" I asked. I was beginning to see that my life required more than my good strong arm and a sword. I didn't have the wherewithal that the women of the sisterhood or even little Casidhea had. Sloane told me I had to know myself, and now I knew I had to become reacquainted with the God my mother sent me to.

Balder stopped his pacing. "Do you want to pray?"

"I don't remember how," I said.

"Kneel, Father. I'll kneel with you." Casidhea was at my side, she pulled on my hand and I went to my knees. She knelt beside me, holding my hand, while Balder prayed.

Friend, I am not a religious man, but I am a God-fearing man. And I know God saw us there and knew he could not let Black Haarald win. And I knelt all because of a little girl. Sloane knew. I heard her soft laugh in the wind. Don't tell me I didn't because I did.

*   *   *

One day from Norns, Black Haarald felt the chill creep into his bones, nothing made him happy now. He derived no pleasure from food, drink, or his consorts. He gazed into mirrored brass to look at his reflection. The face looking back at him could have been Cillian, except for the flaming red hair. The only thing that will appease him is Sloane. He had let her escape once, but not this time.

Sixty-five—Preparation for Battle

Sloane was there when I awoke. She was in earnest conversation with Casidhea. When she saw me awake and sitting up she came to my side. "You're doing well with our daughter. And the defenses and training are good, but will be to no avail against this force. Black Haarald must be separated from his fleet. I've missed you, Raider." She ran her fingers over my face and into my hair. "Black Haarald must be separated. I have told Casidhea what she must do, so do not stop her or overprotect her."

"Will she be in danger?" I asked, pulling my clothes on.

"No. She will be directing the will of all the Sisters on the Island channeled through me, against the fleet of Black Haarald." Sloane looked tired; her words were coming slow.

"Come breakfast with us. After all, we are the Cillian and Casidhea family of Sloane," I said.

Sloane tried to flash one of her mischievous grins, but it didn't work. Casidhea put her arms around her mother and held her while I put some water and fruit in front of her. She nibbled a few bites and laid her head on the table in exhausted sleep. I carried her to my bed and left her to Casidhea's care.

*   *   *

"Balder, make that sea wall two stones higher," I shouted. "Einarr, make those sword cuts deep, like this." I swung my broad sword into the cutting post and cut it off throat high. I walked the length of the cutting post, slicing the tops off all of them. "Now belly cuts, drop the guts out of them."

189

Snorri shouted, "Cillian is back, UUUURRRRAAAAAHHHHH." And old Snorri scythed his old sword through the top of his cutting post. When my crew was through, all the villagers could do was make hamstring cuts on the posts. But the blood was up in Raiders, and we were the ones who would do the killing.

"Still the Raider Cillian, fight well. Be not surprised if you find you are crossing swords with yourself." Sloane stood beside me. How she moved from place to place without being seen moving, I never knew. *I wonder if Casidhea can do this.*

"Yes, our daughter has the moving gift. Cillian, she must be on that promontory with Balder when Black Haarald arrives," Sloane said. "I have so much that I could say, and maybe should say, but I won't. Fight well, my Cillian, even as you fight yourself. I can not, nor can anybody help you in this fight."

I turned from looking at the promontory she pointed to, and I saw the last traces of her, but she was gone. *I wonder was she here at all?* I walked the perimeter, keeping a close watch on Casidhea and Balder as they climbed to the promontory. This fatherhood is difficult, and I have only been doing it for days.

"The fleet." Balder's shout came echoing down from the heights.

Everybody stopped, even I. The fear started and I knew we had to stop it before it became wildfire.

"We'll picnic on the sea wall until Old Black Haarald gets here, bring food," I shouted. And it worked, the people started laughing and moving again. But I was worried. I was going to cross swords with myself, that's what Sloane said.

Sixty-six—Battle

"You hear that?" Einarr said. "Look at the clouds."

There was noise; no, not noise. It was the sound of power, if you can describe power. That is what it sounded like.

Casidhea stood on the promontory surrounded by great billowing thunderheads, lightning flashing in and across them, but there was no thunder. Balder stood beside her; they were illuminated in a golden bubble.

Casidhea moved her arm, and the roiling, flashing heavens advanced out over the sea. Balder watched as waterspouts arched skyward and the large fleet now was tiny, minuscule to the power of Casidhea's storm.

The long boats that carried the mercenaries, hired for this battle, immediately dropped sail and back-watered their oars turning around, there was no profit there. The six remaining long boats of the Skirniri were enveloped. The Skirniri fought as pair bonds, and they manned their boats two to an oar. This unholy bonding produced fierce fighters as they fought to protect the only one they loved other than themselves. Their boats were scattered and tossed, the mast shorn of sails, crackling blue with fire of the thunderheads that walked the masts and jumped from ship to ship. When a Skirniri slipped over the side, immediately his other screamed and jumped in for the same fate.

The one long boat that was untouched by the storm was Black Haarald's. He watched in horror as his fleet was pushed back, scattered and sank.

"Come about. Come about," he shouted. His oarsman strained muscles, popping veins bulging, but the sea and the wind kept the long boat heading for Norns.

Haarald's longboat cut through the water without a

wake; the boat was not moving through the sea. The sea was bringing Haarald to me.

We watched the storm and the one long boat that flew towards us. No words were exchanged; Brundr squatted down, then sprang high in the air and ran in place, knees held high. Snorri grunted and shrugged the fur off his sword arm. Ufr's smile was fearsome as he swung and twirled his axes. I touched not my weapons. I stood feet apart, hands hooked to my belt watching, watching, and praying.

"Archers." Einarr shouted. "Loose."

Men, women, and children had been pressed into service as archers, and the sky was filled with whistling shafts.

The Skirniri dropped their oars and thrust their shields overhead, but they were too late. Half the crew were skewered, those of the pair bond that were spared shrieked their anger and despair. Black Haarald's fear left him and hate; black foul hate gorged his already filthy soul. The second flight claimed few victims, and there was no time for the third; the long boat flew on the shore.

"Spears on the wall." Men, women, and children dropped bows, picked up their spears, and took positions on the wall.

I stood with my crew waiting. The long boat settled, canted to the beach; it was porcupined with arrows. From inside came a keening wail of evil, deep black screeching.

The hairs stood up on my body. What kind of evil was this? And over the sides, they spilled. Bodies painted black and red, shaven heads and mouths open wide in that diabolic scream.

"UUUUUURRRRRRRRRRAAAAAAAAAHH HHHHH!" rose from the throats of my raiders, slowly

192

gathering momentum. Then my seven trotted, spreading out because they were still seven against two score. As their cry rose, they ran, crashing into three Skirniri. First was Old Snorri; he chopped down two before Brundr was at his side, he dispatched the third without breaking stride.

I stood back watching as my raiders, true berserkers left the beach littered with decapitated and disemboweled Skirniri. Then standing to be seen, a warrior, the only one left on the long boat. My heart thudded into extra beats; this had to be Black Haarald. He jumped down, landing on both feet, knees bent. Straightening he looked at his dead lying at his feet and covering the beach. Then he turned his gaze on my seven; they were not even breathing hard, just leaning on swords and axes, watching this new threat.

Einarr, without turning to me, shouted, "I'll take him?"

"No, Cillian kills this one." I fastened my eyes on this warrior, watching every move, looking for a weakness.

Haarald turned his gaze on me, disdainfully turning his back on my crew. He wore his long sword like I did, over his back. He reached over his shoulder and swept it free.

Swinging the blade like a cat swishes its tail, he came to me, walking knees bent, he had fought before.

I just stood and watched and did not draw. This man was going to be my toughest opponent yet. "Haarald, remove your helm, let me see your face."

Haarald stopped. I removed my helm, causing him to step forward, looking hard. Then he stuck the sword in the sand and pulled his helm off. The first thing was a great mop of fire red hair, but the face made my heart stop, my left knee loosened.

193

The high forehead with brow shrouding the eyes, his nose almost pug, his cheeks smooth and clear, mouth thin and straight, chin strong. My hand went to the scar that ran from my left eye to jaw line, then found the scar on my lower lip, the nose broken more than once. I was looking at a good-looking version of myself.

My sword skeeled out of its scabbard. Haarald drew his out of the sand, we threw the helms aside and advanced on each other.

"I wondered why I picked this face," Haarald said, his blade again swishing back and forth slicing the air. "Now you can watch as you kill yourself."

The town's people and my crew were on all sides of us. I saw Balder and Casidhea directly behind Haarald. "Balder, take her from here."

"No, I'll not go," Casidhea screamed. Balder looked on helplessly.

Black Haarald turned to the scream, knowing I would not kill him from behind. My raiders quickly inserted themselves in protective screen for Casidhea. Black Haarald turned his fire head toward me, leaving all who saw his face in fear and wonderment, like I was.

"Where is Sloane? I'll have her whelp after I have her." His face—my face—glowed with evil.

I was holding my sword loosely, but backhanded it and sliced his left cheek from eye to jaw line. Stepping in close, I brought my left fist down on his nose, pulping it like a pomegranate. No shouts, only grunts with the effort of the blows. He staggered back and brought his point up. A great cheer went up from the crowd.

Black Haarald shook his head, blood sprayed from nose and cheek, a smile came across my face, the one I'd just cut, and it chilled me. "So you're Cillian, the Raider?"

He crossed his arms and shimmering, almost disappearing, reappeared as two, the crowd moaned.

"Father, whatever he can do, so can you. Try, Father try," I heard Casidhea scream.

I felt Sloane beside me; I felt my quivering becoming liquid, then I heard the crowd shout, "Cillian is two."

I, we, turned our swords on the Black Haarald's. The steel rang and clashed, sparks showered us. As we fought, I felt Black Haarald entering my mind, his evil was eating away my strength. "Fight him with sword and thought; use your Mother and the Island." I heard Sloane, she must be there.

One part of me in the two of me fought with sword cutting and thrusting. The other part drew upon the womb and my mother. Cillian the Raider would not win, but Nial Champion of the Island would.

I pushed into Haarald's mind, searching for his soul. Clangggg, scccchhh, the blades rang. Ungh, we grunted, and I pushed deeper. Then he hesitated, his eyes registering surprise. "So you're more powerful than I thought. You attack on two fronts."

I felt the evil swell and pulsate as it tried to feed on me. But I was in the Gossamer womb of my mother, taking strength from her. She gave as all mothers give strength to those they nurture. I felt the renewing power swell my heart, mind, and body.

Now I fought, knowing the outcome just as Black Haarald knew he was vanquished, his sword was weaker, his feet too heavy to pick up.

In a mighty flash and with the screeching sound of evil dying, the other me finished the other Haarald; both vanished. Haarald stopped, his arms dropped; he fell to his knees head bowed. Vanquished.

I grounded my long blade in the sand, pulled Black

Haarald's head back by the red hair baring his throat. His face, my face now more than ever the slashed cheek, the broken nose. I hesitated. **"Kill him,"** the crowd roared.

I stopped my cut, "Casidhea, bind him with some of your hair." I would not kill.

Without questioning me, my Casidhea cut a plait from her head and bound Haarald's hands. "It's done, Father."

"Balder, Einarr, dispose of the bodies, celebrate after cleaning the beach." The words came as a shout that was not loud but was heard by all.

*   *   *

Sixty-seven—Changes at the Shrine

"Come, Casidhea, bring Haarald, we go to your shrine." Haarald stood and lead out as if he knew where the shrine was.

Casidhea put her little hand in mine. "I'm glad you didn't kill him."

I squeezed her hand, "I don't know why I didn't," I said. "I wish Sloane were here to tell me what to do."

"What were you going to do with Haarald?" she asked, her little legs working to keep up.

I slowed down and Haarald, sensing the pace change, slowed too. "I think Haarald will spend the rest of his years in the Shrine as caretaker," I said. Now when did I decide this? I'd really rather just cut his throat and be done with it. I'd like to make him hurt for all the hurts he did Sloane.

The Shrine was old; the only way you could tell it was

a shrine was by the flowers, and greenery around the entrance. Carved into the rock was a graceful woman holding out a hand in welcome. Haarald stopped cold, collapsing and shaking crying like a woman. I didn't know what to do; this certainly wasn't the Haarald I had fought.

Casidhea knelt beside him. "Come help me, get him in the Shrine," she said, helping him to his feet.

I hurried to help; it seemed that he was shrinking, his clothes were hanging on him. Inside the temple I picked him up and laid him on the offering table.

"Loosen his clothing. Father."

I undid the belt, unbuckled the buckler, undid the linen tunic undergarment, and quickly closed it.

"What is the matter? Is there a wound?" Casidhea asked.

"You look, daughter, you are skilled in the healing arts," I said, stepping out of the way.

Casidhea stepped up to the still form. "Father, those wounds you gave him are healed, gone." She opened the undergarment and revealed what I had seen. Haarald had breasts. "Father, we have to look further," Casidhea said, raising the bottom of the under tunic. "Haarald is a woman," she said.

I saw the evidence, and even though I had trouble at the entrance of the womb on the island, I knew what a woman looked like, and Haarald was a beautiful woman. "He looks like Sloane," I said.

"What did you say, Father?"

"I wish Sloane was here," I said.

"Call her," Casidhea said. "No, no need. Hello, Mother."

I whirled around. "Sloane." She stood softly, indistinctly in the shadows, saying nothing, not moving. Then the room bloomed with light and as abruptly became shadowed again. Sloane moved to me and held me with a hello kiss, then swept Casidhea in her arms, laughing and hugging.

"You did well, little daughter, you did well." Sloane turned to me. "Cillian, didn't our daughter do well?"

"Yes, she did. I should have told her. Casidhea, I'm proud of you." *What about me? Didn't I do good too?*

Sloane stood, "Oh, Cillian, still the little boy, you did well." And she kissed me properly.

After a couple of heady seconds, I broke the embrace. "Sloane, Haarald is a woman, and he—she looks like you except for her face; it looks like me."

"Look again, Cillian."

And as I looked, and this is no sailor's lie, Haarald's face softened, the faint marks of my cuts and the pugged-up nose became Sloane's. His—er, her eyes blended into high cheekbones and downy soft skin, her ears peeked through hair that still flamed like the setting sun.

"Who is this, Mother?" Casidhea asked.

I continued to watch Haarald as his body changed, refining itself to the item that I was looking at. It was almost as if I was molding him-her to look like Sloane. In the background I heard Sloane say, "Haarald is Hallveig; she is my sister. Od was my father too." Sloane stroked Hallveig's hair and cheek. "She does look like me, doesn't she, Cillian?"

"What's she going to act like?" was all I said. I still think my thoughts had something to do with the way Hallveig now looked.

"Cillian, your thoughts did shape Hallveig because you, Casidhea, and Hallveig are linked together now."

Sloane turned to us, "Come grasp her hands on either side and join yours across her."

Casidhea quickly picked up Hallveig's hand and looked at me. "Come on, Father."

I stood where I was, something was happening. I did not like it. "Sloane, if I do this, how will I change?"

"Cillian, you were never the simple raider were you? Your dream of searching and not knowing what you were searching for; do this and your search is over." Sloane took my hand and placed Hallveig's in it. I looked at Casidhea holding out her hand for me to take.

"Sloane, I don't want to forget you. If I do this, grant me the memory of you."

"You won't entirely forget me, Cillian. I have loved you." I grasped Casidhea's hand and . . .

Sixty-eight—Green Isle and Home

The sea was running with us; the sails hummed with the wind, I stood at the tiller watching Balder and Casidhea sorting through the medicines in their bags. Einarr and the crew were repairing ropes and generally taking it easy.

"Cillian, make room for me, and Nial." Hallveig very pretty and very pregnant, made her way to the tiller seat.

"You don't know that it will be a boy. What if it's a girl?" I moved and she slipped by, touching me as she knew I liked to be touched.

"If it is a girl, what would we name her?"

"Sloane, the name Sloane runs through my head all the time," I said. "We will make The Green Isle tonight, love, and Sloane can be born there."

I know you say how can I tell you this tale when all memory was wiped out when we grasped hands. Friend, when a man loves a woman, his mind may get crowded with memories, but he would never forget a ginger-haired Sloane.

This is not the end of Sloane and Cillian; one final adventure follows.

the room bloomed with light and as abruptly became shadowed again. Sloane moved to me and held me with a hello kiss, then swept Casidhea in her arms, laughing and hugging.

"You did well, little daughter, you did well." Sloane turned to me. "Cillian, didn't our daughter do well?"

"Yes, she did. I should have told her. Casidhea, I'm proud of you." *What about me? Didn't I do good too?*

Sloane stood, "Oh, Cillian, still the little boy, you did well." And she kissed me properly.

After a couple of heady seconds, I broke the embrace. "Sloane, Haarald is a woman, and he—she looks like you except for her face; it looks like me."

"Look again, Cillian."

And as I looked, and this is no sailor's lie, Haarald's face softened, the faint marks of my cuts and the pugged-up nose became Sloane's. His—er, her eyes blended into high cheekbones and downy soft skin, her ears peeked through hair that still flamed like the setting sun.

"Who is this, Mother?" Casidhea asked.

I continued to watch Haarald as his body changed, refining itself to the item that I was looking at. It was almost as if I was molding him-her to look like Sloane. In the background I heard Sloane say, "Haarald is Hallveig; she is my sister. Od was my father too." Sloane stroked Hallveig's hair and cheek. "She does look like me, doesn't she, Cillian?"

"What's she going to act like?" was all I said. I still think my thoughts had something to do with the way Hallveig now looked.

"Cillian, your thoughts did shape Hallveig because you, Casidhea, and Hallveig are linked together now."

a shrine was by the flowers, and greenery around the entrance. Carved into the rock was a graceful woman holding out a hand in welcome. Haarald stopped cold, collapsing and shaking crying like a woman. I didn't know what to do; this certainly wasn't the Haarald I had fought.

Casidhea knelt beside him. "Come help me, get him in the Shrine," she said, helping him to his feet.

I hurried to help; it seemed that he was shrinking, his clothes were hanging on him. Inside the temple I picked him up and laid him on the offering table.

"Loosen his clothing. Father."

I undid the belt, unbuckled the buckler, undid the linen tunic undergarment, and quickly closed it.

"What is the matter? Is there a wound?" Casidhea asked.

"You look, daughter, you are skilled in the healing arts," I said, stepping out of the way.

Casidhea stepped up to the still form. "Father, those wounds you gave him are healed, gone." She opened the undergarment and revealed what I had seen. Haarald had breasts. "Father, we have to look further," Casidhea said, raising the bottom of the under tunic. "Haarald is a woman," she said.

I saw the evidence, and even though I had trouble at the entrance of the womb on the island, I knew what a woman looked like, and Haarald was a beautiful woman. "He looks like Sloane," I said.

"What did you say, Father?"

"I wish Sloane was here," I said.

"Call her," Casidhea said. "No, no need. Hello, Mother."

I whirled around. "Sloane." She stood softly, indistinctly in the shadows, saying nothing, not moving. Then